Destiny of Unspoken Words

Nathan L. Jarrett

Copyright @2015

Nathan L. Jarrett

All rights reserved. No part of this book may be reproduced or transmitted in any form or by any means, electronic or mechanical, including photocopying, recording, or by any information storage and retrieval system, without permission in writing from the copyright owner or author.

The information in this book is for educational purposes only.

ISBN-13: 978-1516993055
ISBN-10: 1516993055

Second Edition
Published; August 2015
Jarrett Publications
Printed in the United States of America

Table of Contents

Table of Contents iii
Forward iv
Preface iv
Introduction v
Chapter 1 1
Chapter 2 6
Chapter 3 10
Chapter 4 28
Chapter 5 34
Chapter 6 54
Chapter 7 64
Chapter 8 70
Chapter 9 76
Chapter 10 82
Chapter 11 88
Chapter 12 97
Chapter 13 101
Chapter 14 109
Chapter 15 117
Chapter 16 128
Chapter 17 133
Chapter 18 147

Forward

I have been greatly blessed by several of the people that God has brought into my life. I have had a few outstanding supervisors whom I also count as friends that deserve (both now and in the future) credit for my work. They have not only trained me, but allowed me to grow beyond my training. I am thankful for this opportunity and for the value it has added to my life. I challenge every reader to do as Nathan has taught me and challenged me to do both through this book and conversation - Take conscious control of your own destiny.

Lisa Goodwin

Preface

I want to thank Lisa Goodwin for all of her time put into proofing this book. Her passion for doing things right the first time shows up in her work. It is so very refreshing to work with a proofreader who has a passion for what they do. She does her best in everything that she does. She feels that if she is not pleased with the result, no one else should be pleased with it either.

Introduction

The journey of life is met with many detours, hurdles, crossroads, and free passes. Each one constitutes an experience. Those experiences, when reflected upon, can change the course of your life. How you interpret those events in your life defines who you are. The title behind your name, the car you drive, the neighborhood in which you live, how much is in your bank account, and many other benchmarks will *never* define who you are.

Destiny is defined as the inevitable or necessary fate to which a particular person or thing is destined; one's lot. He learned to control his through CHOICES. Who controls your *destiny?*

Chapter 1

A man is driving down the interstate highway in his BMW. The day was turning to dusk. He soon approached an exit ramp for Mayfield Road and exited the highway. He turned westbound and drove down the four-lane street of the small town. He approached the restaurant he was looking for and parked in front of it.

The building was a rustic brick in color. The sign out front says, "Samuel's Natural Organics Dinner and Eats." He glanced inside through one of two large windows and noticed there were quite a few people inside. However, that was normal even though it was slightly beyond dinnertime. So, this six foot one, blonde man got out of his car and looked around. He was well dressed in casual clothes, and his hair was well groomed. His facial features were that of a male model. He walked through the front door of the restaurant.

He stopped by the sign that said; "Please wait to be seated." The owner walked by and noticed him.

"Hi, Brent! How are things with you my friend? I haven't seen you in a week or so."

The owner and Brent shook hands.

"Hello, Ceasario! Nice to see you. I've been busy, but I thought I'd stop by and grab something to eat. How are things with you and the family?"

"Oh, things are fine. Business is great - maybe too great. Always busy, but I'm not complaining. The wife is fine. And I'm going to be a nonno again! That will make number nine. Hopin' for at least one more to make it an even ten!"

"Well congratulations to you 'Nonno'. May you be blessed with all of your life's desires. Now, what is today's special?"

Ceasario thought for a moment…

Ceasario was from Italy. He was from the old country and old school thinking. He believed life should be centered around family and food. He immigrated here decades ago and built a chain of organic restaurants, which is the second largest chain in the country. He liked his employees to call him 'Pops'. This 5' 7" grey haired man had that likeable personality - everyone who knew him just loved him.

He continued; "Is it just you or is someone else joining you ... you know whata' I mean..."

"It's just me tonight. Maybe someday..."

"I fix you somethin'. It'll be a surprise for you, ok? You know I have good organic food here that is healthy for you."

"That will be fine, Ceasario. That's why I eat here - because you have great food!"

"Come over and sit. I'll have waitress bring you out something before main course. She will be right over."

Ceasario disappeared into the kitchen and Brent sat down. About five minutes later, the waitress came over and brought him a few appetizers and something to drink.

"Hi, Brent. Haven't seen you in a while. How are things going?"

"Things are fine, Cheryl. Thanks for asking."

"Here are your usual appetizers. Are these ok? Oh, and Pops said he's fixing you something special. You know how he is..."

"Yes I do Cheryl. This is just great! Thank you!"

"If you need anything else, let me know." She said with a smile as she walked away.

Eventually his dinner came and was consumed in an orderly fashion. He paid his bill and left.

He got into his car and pushed the button to start it. The car roared to life. Brent paused for a few minutes just staring at the dashboard blankly. He finally put it in gear, backed up, and drove off.

The drive home was quite interesting. His thoughts raced back to Cheryl. She reminded him of someone. As he remembered her words, his thoughts and feelings took a different turn.

As he drove back to the entrance ramp of the expressway

on the four-lane road, Brent began to realize those thoughts and feelings that were deep inside were beginning to surface in a completely different way.

He opened the moon roof to get a gentle breeze in the car. As he drove down the highway, the car got up to speed quickly, as usual. However, what was unusual was the fact that Brent wasn't paying much attention to the enjoyment his car gave him. This was rare for Brent. In his car, he always took the long road because it's such a blast to drive!

He glanced down at the clock to check the time. It was 8:00 pm and it was dark. Autumn was here now. *Where did the summer go? It's nearly October. I enjoy the warmth of the summer days. Wearing shorts and tight-fitting T-shirts... Showing off a little? Maybe. What am I going on about? Well, soon my Grace will be here. Grace!*

He looked down at the speedometer that lit up into a beautiful amber color against the black background. He realized he was going 82 in a 65. *Oh boy, that's not going to work.*

As he slowed the vehicle to the speed limit, his mind drifted again to the night's events. He wondered for a brief moment if Grace would actually make the trip. *By all her emails, I don't think that will be a problem. Ah, she's about five foot six with those blue eyes of hers. And that natural honey blonde hair...* He sighed aloud. *Wow! Even her name, Grace, is fitting for her.*

He drove past a major hotel along the highway. He instantly thought of the reservations he had made for her at the hotel in town. The hotel was very new and looked great. It had an entrance of grandeur with two sandy-colored stone pillars that looked like two soldiers standing guard at the gate. Intricately chiseled above both pillars were people dancing, eating, and sleeping. It gave a sheltered feeling to those that entered the hotel. Ultimately, it conveyed a touch of class.

Hopefully she'll be comfortable there. Only the best I

can give her will do, well to a point. Maybe I should have some flowers put in the room before she gets there ... hmmm, just one red rose so she knows I'm thoughtful and was looking after the little things to make her comfortable and welcome here. I can drop it off the day before or have a florist deliver it to the room before she gets there.

He changed lanes and adjusted himself in his seat. *I wonder if Grace might get the wrong impression and feel a little uncomfortable. I don't want her to think I'm romancing her just to bed her. Maybe I should use a pink rose, or better yet a yellow rose, for friendship. I would never play around with a women's heart like that. It's too delicate and precious to be abusing. She's such a sweet person. It instantly brings tears to my eyes thinking of the first time we met. I can see and feel the void and pain in that beautiful heart of hers over the tragedy of her child's death.*

Brent reflected on his own trauma with the sudden death of his child and how he could help Grace.

All I would like to do is comfort her the way I wanted to be comforted. Even if it's just to sit, listen to her vent, and shed some tears. I'd like to wipe those tears off her cheek when they start to fall if she would let me. I feel she needs to be comforted so much. I bet the pain and the sorrow she has learned to endure is so deep that it might come out the other end of the earth if it could. On the other hand, I have to balance those feelings with the ones of happiness and elation at the chance of being able to see her again. Just thinking about her taking her valuable time to visit and the moments we will be sharing together makes me feel warm inside. Grace has this charm about her that can't be explained. It must be experienced. I really wonder if that is one of her greatest attributes. One just has to experience it to understand it. Hmmm, maybe I can write a poem just for her ... about her and have a maid lay it on the bed so she can read it before she drifts off to sleep.

Brent continued to ponder. *Should I write it now or*

maybe I'll wait until after her visit? I could point out all the great things that she is. I really don't know her that well yet. However, I feel something is there ... something that my heart wants ... yearns for, deep inside me. I think I'll wait until after she leaves. I'll know her a little bit better then, and she will appreciate the poem more because of the intimate time we spend together.

Brent started to remember and reminisce about all the times they talked in the parking lot after the support group meetings. The meetings were there just to support the parents and siblings who have had a child die.

It takes so many years for many to get any type of a handle on dealing with this kind of loss. However, all the times at the meetings, I saw a glow and a shine in her eyes. It's interesting I noticed that light in her eyes back then. Grace always had a certain glow that radiated out and would seem somewhat mystical in its power in that it seemed to draw a person into it, yet keep them at a distance too. Could she have been attracted to me back then? ... Nah.

Brent turned off onto a ramp to another highway. He moved through the turns and headed east.

Heading east. Hmmm, doesn't heading east in some folk lore mean attaining new knowledge and new beginnings? Maybe this will bring a new beginning to my life!!!

I remember in those days so many years ago, how much I admired her for going through what she did, and yet she could be so gentle and glowing at the same time. I know how hard it was for me during those years. I wondered a few times if I had helped her and comforted her with our little talks. I would sure like to give her one of those hugs that says, 'Hey; I'm here. Go ahead and let it out! I care, so just take your time!! I'm in no hurry!!!' To hold her tight, so she feels secure. To brush away the hair from her pretty face as its tilted forward so that those negative emotions come flowing out. What I wouldn't give to gently lift her face and tenderly wipe away the tears that represent the pain that tortures her soul. Hoping that with each stroke across her face, she will absorb my energy and use it to help her cope with this traumatic experience. That's what sharing your life is all about, I believe ... being there for one another through the good, and the challenging times. I can't imagine what it would be like to warmly receive the same from her in return. I wonder if our relationship would be so unique as to not talk about the same topic twice. I can't wait to hear her voice again - so gentle and soothing. The sincerity that flowed forth was something that I haven't felt with any other people. Being a service technician, I deal with people all the time. So I understand people and the energy they give off when they speak. I have to chuckle. I wonder if her little humor and wit is just as good in person as it is in the emails! It's probably better.

Chapter 2

He started to realize it was a typical, cool late September day. He set the climate control to 74 degrees. *Gosh, I like these controls. I hope she enjoys the car. It has a romantic flair to it. It has "his and her" side controls.*

He enjoyed the ride with contented thoughts of her to keep him company. *Ahhh, this is the life. Now if only I had someone to share it with...*

As his thoughts about her continued, his smile grew wider. He turned and looked as a car pulled up next to him, passenger side, on the highway. It was a beautiful silver Jag. The gleaming car was unmistakable as it passed under a bright highway light.

Hmmm, it seems like someone wants to race on this stretch of highway. It's probably some rich yuppie kid, maybe a punk, out for a thrill ride. Or maybe he's on his way to the opera ... yeah, right. Brent chuckled a bit.

As he looked closer, he saw through the window an attractive 50ish redhead driving. *Well now, let's have some*

FUN with this situation.
Brent pushed the button to roll down the front passenger-side window. To his astonishment, 'Redhead' rolled her driver's side window down too. *This is going to be interesting. Should I or shouldn't I? ... Yes, I should.*
Brent yelled out in a chivalrous voice, "IN YOUR DREAMS, LADY. GET THAT PIECE OF TRASH OFF THE ROAD!"
He chuckled, waved farewell, and raced off. The G force from the acceleration pushed him back in his seat hard. Brent noticed her car accelerating as she tried to catch up to him, but she quickly gave up the chase and skulked off at the next exit.
He slowed the car down. *That felt so good. I've always wanted to say that, but never found myself in the right situation. Nice shot of adrenalin! I never believed other BMW owners when they talked about a car that purrs under your touch. But now, I'm a believer! Hmmm, maybe I should grow up a little bit? Act my age? Exhibit my wisdom? Nah, I'm alone. No one's around. Acting like an adult is no fun. Occasionally, you have to let go and let the inner child out.*
That broke his concentration about Grace for a few minutes. But it didn't take long before thoughts of her beautiful shoulder length, golden blonde hair drifted back. *I practically salivated over the photo she emailed to me! Gosh, is Grace beautiful. Gorgeous is more like it! I can't get over how much better she looks since I last saw her. She is so radiant in that photo.*
Again, his thoughts parked in the lot of his mind where he could think of her ... hope and dream of what might lie ahead for the coming weekend.
Will Grace have a great time and be comfortable too? Gosh, I hope with all my heart. Hmmm... maybe she'll want to leave early. No, no, don't think that way. Think positive. She's nothing like Sue. Sue terrorized me every way possible for so many years, and I allowed it. But Sue's gone now. So

relax, and remember how perfect Graces hugs are - so pure and genuine. No other hug has ever comforted me like that. Keep focusing on the positive and the possibilities to come...

Brent desperately wanted her sitting next to him in the car. *If I wish hard enough, could I make it happen? Just to have her caring heart and soul nearby so I can feel her energy would bring bliss into my heart. If I could only turn my head and peer into her eyes, as they tell a story of great love and great pain. Would her eyes glimmer like the star-filled sky on a clear and quiet night? Would the night appear brighter just from the reflection of the dash lights in her eyes? Ahhh. If I could have only one wish, it would be to have Grace sitting right here. Gosh, my heart aches to share this with her. Can I safely think it without jinxing it? Yes, I control my destiny. Therefore, I would say to her...*

Suddenly, he was startled by a sound that cut through his thoughts. There it was again! The sound jerked him back to reality. It was his cell phone.

Who the heck is calling me at this time of night? Maybe it's her. Coincidence? I gave her my phone numbers in an email. Wouldn't it be a sign that we were on the same wavelength?

He searched for his cell phone and found it in his jacket pocket. He pulled it out and checked the caller ID. *Hmmm... the number doesn't look familiar.*

"Hello?"

"Sam?" the female voice on the other end inquired.

Brent hoped that it was Grace. But, by the sound of the voice, he was pretty sure it wasn't her.

"You must have the wrong number ma'am." Brent answered back.

"Oh, sorry." And there was nothing but a dial tone.

Brent absentmindedly flipped the phone onto the passenger's seat.

As Brent cruised down the highway, he realized he needed something to drink. He came to the next exit and turned off. As he reached the top of the ramp, he thought… *Hmmm, to the left, fast-food restaurants - the world of hydrogenated oils. To the right, a truck stop, with fine gum chomping service. Decisions, decisions. I'm not in the mood for truck stop hospitality, so left it is. Even if the restaurants are a ways down the road, it beats having to stare at a middle-aged woman with makeup to spare asking, 'what'll it be?'*

The car accelerated down the road. The streetlights started to shine inside the car a little faster each time he passed under them due to the increase in speed. Then, the streetlights disappeared. He started to focus on the car and the ride it was giving him. *Ah. What can I say? This is the life! If Grace was here, I wonder which choice she would have made.*

His thoughts started to drift when suddenly in the rearview mirror, Brent noticed a car hugging his bumper. *Oh great, a tailgater. He could use the left lane. So why hang out behind me?*

As if in answer to his question, red-flashing lights appeared on top of the car. "OH NO!" he said out loud. His heart jumped and raced like mad. His hands started to tremble and sweat. He looked down at the speedometer. *I'm doing fifty two in a thirty five mph zone. Well, I guess I'm getting a ticket.* Brent turned on his signal and found a flat area on the side of the road.

His car came to a stop on the side of the road and the squad car pulled over behind him. The officer's spotlight pointing inside Brent's car startled him. *It's been a while since I've been pulled over.* He is managing to keep his composure through it all.

He didn't move much because he didn't want to startle the officer. The squad car door opened, and the officer stepped out and put on his hat. *Well, it's either the county police or a state trooper.*

As the officer slowly approached Brent's car, Brent

noticed that it looked like a county sheriff. The area was not very well lit and with the light from the squad car behind him, it was difficult to make out any of the officer's features other than the hat he was wearing. The only thing he could notice was that the officer didn't appear to be overweight. Brent pushed the button to roll the windows down as the officer approached his car. He observed a brief flash of light coming from the officer's face. With the officer's next step, Brent saw the mirrored sunglasses and thought, *who wears mirrored sunglasses at night?*

Chapter 3

As the officer slowly approached the car, Brent noticed a flashlight in his left hand and his right hand resting on his weapon. "Sir, can I see your driver's license, vehicle registration, and proof of insurance?' He politely asked.

"Of course, officer."

He slowly reached into his front pocket to get his wallet out. (He has carried his wallet in his front pocket ever since he went to a female chiropractor many years ago. While she was adjusting him once, she gave him a little whack on the butt and told him to put his wallet in his front pocket. She said that carrying it in his back pocket could knock his spine out of adjustment a little bit. It was strange, but ever since then, he has kept his wallet in his front pocket.) He opened his wallet and handed his license to the officer. The officer shined the flashlight onto the driver's license.

"I'll get the registration and the insurance card. They're in the glove box." He noticed the officer step back a half step. He transferred the license to his left hand between his index and second finger and then placed his right hand on his service revolver. Brent carefully got the other two articles out and handed them to the officer. "Ok, Mr. ... Ramies. Is this your current address?" he asked politely.

"Yes."

"Wait here. I'll be right back."

Yeah, like I'm going anywhere. Brent watched the officer in both the rear and the side view mirrors as he went back to his car.

The officer got into his unit. Brent could faintly hear him talking on his radio. After what seemed to be a long time, the officer's car door opened and he got out. He made his way to Brent's car. "Are you from around here, Mr. Ramies?"

"I've lived here since July of 1995."

"Have you ever lived in Illinois, Mr. Ramies?"

"Yes, I have."

"What part of Illinois, sir?"

Hmmm... something strange is going on here. What does that have to do with whether I get a ticket or not? Brent thought.

"Northeast part of the state in a town called Rolling Meadows. Why do you ask, officer?"

The officer took three steps back and said, "Ok, Mr. Ramies. Slowly get out of the car, sir!"

Oh, this is GREAT! I'm going to jail for sure. Reckless driving, I bet? I'm not drinking. What do you bet he doesn't like people who own German sports cars? His mind raced as he slowly got out of his car.

"Now, Mr. Ramies, put your hands on the car and spread your feet apart."

Brent complied with his instructions. The officer continued to give Brent instructions on what to do, which he followed to a tee. He frisked Brent to check for weapons.

"Ok, Mr. Ramies, place your left hand behind your head and keep your right hand on the car."

My gosh. They'll lock me up and throw away the key for sure. What about my car? She hasn't seen it yet. What if I'm still in jail when she calls and I can't answer? This is great, absolutely great!

The police officer proceeded to put handcuffs on Brent's left wrist. Then he slowly spun Brent's right arm down until it reached his lower back.

"Lean forward on the car, sir, until your chest rests on the vehicle." Brent got a good look inside his car because the moon roof was open. *Hmmm... there's a little bit of dirt inside it. Why should I be worried about that right now?*

The officer then proceeded to lock Brent's right wrist in the handcuffs. Now both hands were locked together behind his back. "Ok, Mr. Ramies, turn around and lean back on the car."

Brent did as he was told. The officer turned Brent around and leaned his back against the car. As he was turning around, a strange feeling came over Brent. He hadn't seen or heard a passing car since he was pulled over. He felt a touch of terror run down his spine.

Brent started to reflect on an experience from a long time ago. He felt sheer terror at three different times in his life. The first time was when his daughter was rushed to the hospital. Then again, when the operation performed in an attempt to save her life took over twice as long as it was expected to last. The next time was when he got the call from the hospital telling him that all hope was gone and that they would wait for him to come before turning off the breathing machine, he felt fear of unknown proportions.

The third time was when he arrived at the hospital, they were waiting for him at her bedside. Brent remembered the doctor explaining that they had a choice of pushing the button that would stop the machine or having a member of the hospital staff do it. His wife said that she couldn't do it and left the room.

The doctors were on both sides of him holding onto his arms very gently. He looked at the door that his wife had just walked through.

"Mr. Ramies?" one of the doctors asked.

Brent kept looking at the closed door.

"Mr. Ramies?" the doctor asked again. This time he gave a gentle tug on Brent's arm.

Brent was in a slight trance, still staring at the closed door.

"Huh?" There was a pause.

"It's time, sir… if you don't want to push the button, then we will do it for you..."

Brent looked into the eyes of the doctor and then turned his head to his daughter.

Brent paused for a moment and said;

"I'll push the button."

The doctor was taken aback by the decision.

The doctor paused and asked,

"Mr. Ramies, may I ask why you want to do this? It's so very rare that a parent will turn off the machine."

Brent just stood there at the end of her hospital bed, looking at his baby's body lying there. There was a silence so enormous that any noise in the area was masked or sucked out by it. Then he finally said,

"I helped bring her into this world. I held her, cared for her, love her, helped rear her, feed her…" He paused then continued.

"I made a promise to her when she was first brought into the hospital. I told her…" he paused as tears started to flow down his cheeks, but continued as his voice was crackling as all the emotions started to pour out of him.

"I told her I would be with her through all of this, even to the end if need be… I have to keep my promise."

The battle hardened nurses with years of experience and the doctors whom were standing all around her bed had either tears streaming down their cheeks or were sobbing almost uncontrollably.

The doctor standing next to him gave a look and a nod to turn off the breathing machine that kept his daughter alive. He told her he loved her and was sorry for all this. But, there was nothing to be sorry about. It was just fate and it was meant to be, or that's what he told himself. Then the tears flowed so heavily that all he could see were blurry reflections of light. Memories of "I love you, Daddy!"... The times he was by her bedside when she was sick flooded his mind and soul at that moment. The times when he would hug her and she would say, "Thank you for caring for me, Daddy." He gave her so much of his heart and soul... He felt it was a privilege just to be her dad. But that was all gone now. He remembered all the tubes that were like garden hoses sticking out of her chest after the heart surgery and thought how she must have suffered.

Then the floods of "what if's" were released. What if he waited and she got better? What if he prayed harder? What if they found a cure? All the "what if's" continued to flow. Despite his mind's doubts, the doctors, trained experts, said there was no chance. He gave it over to God. *God must want my child and who am I to say 'no' or delay the inevitably.*

She didn't want to live that way. We both did not want to watch her suffer. Without hesitation, he walked over to her side and tenderly whispered into his child's ear, "I love you and I'm sorry." And, with those last spoken words, he pushed the button that ended her life. Part of his heart and life died right there - never to be healed again. He felt something give inside his heart like a rubber band that was stretched so thin that it had snapped. His life would never be the same again. His baby was gone...

Suddenly, Brent was no longer afraid. *Maybe it's my turn? Maybe this officer will end my suffering and what's left of my life. So whatever he is going to dish out, bring it on. It pales in comparison to the real pain I deal with everyday.*

Brent's concentration was broken when the officer said, "Stay here." He walked to his squad car, turned off his spotlight and flashing lights, but left his head lights on. The officer stood about six feet tall. Even with his uniform on, he had a striking muscular physique. He took off his hat and flung it onto the hood of his squad car.

As he slowly walked back, Brent began to recognize a familiarity with his facial silhouette. The officer, now standing three feet in front of Brent, said, "You hotrod drivers are all alike. You don't remember me do you, Mister?"

Brent still couldn't make out his facial features because of the dark. The officer removed his sunglasses and said, "Does that help you, Mr. Ramies?"

Brent felt a cold breeze going down the back of his neck. The officer got close enough for Brent to be able to make out his facial features. Something about his voice started to sound familiar, something from the past… but he still couldn't place the voice or the face.

In what seemed like slow motion, the officer took a step back with his right leg and placed his right hand on the holster, which held his service revolver. With his thumb, he unsnapped the leather strap that held the deadly weapon at bay.

Well now, isn't this an incredible predicament! Who from my past have I injured or hurt? Who would want to harm me? It seems like just when something good is about to happen in my life, misfortune takes the upper hand. Well, if this is my destiny, then so be it.

Brent's breathing relaxed to small shallow breaths. *Well, I might as well close my eyes and hope it happens fast so I don't suffer for very long.* It became so quiet that it seemed he was in a vacuum. Amazingly, he wasn't afraid and was at peace.

Hmmm. Maybe I should sing as I make my way to the pearly gates. Oh, how I long to look upon the face of my precious angel. So he waited for what seemed like an eternity. Then suddenly, he heard a BANG and a whisper in his ear. He didn't feel anything. He waited for the pain to start. *Maybe if he shot me in the head in just the right place, there won't be any pain. I'll just black out and that's it. I'm off into the afterlife.*

He waited, and waited for the pain or the blackness that starts when someone dies, but nothing happened except for the whispering in his ear. He thought he should listen to it. *Maybe it's God or an angel giving me directions on what to do next seeing I'm in the afterlife now.*

As the whispering continued, he started to recognize the voice. *Gosh, where have I heard that voice before? Wait a minute, wait one blessed minute. I know that jerk. It's my old college buddy. What's his name? George, what's his last name? Atwood... something. Atkins... George Atkins.*

As he started to realize what was happening, Brent still kept hearing the whispering. "Gotcha! I knew some day I'd see you again!"

My gosh. I'm not sure what to do. I can't speak. Should I hug him or beat the crap out of him for scaring me almost to death. I just relived my life in a brief moment, and he's laughing over there.

He heard the laughter coming from his long-time friend. Then he heard the sound of keys rattling in his hand. "Turn around, Brent. Let me get those cuffs off your hands before you mess them up."

Mess them up? What in the world is he trying to say? I'll give him messed up...

As George removed the cuffs, Brent felt relieved.

"Hey, what was the noise that sounded like a gunshot, George?" he asked.

"My unit does that every so often. I'm taking it in on Monday to have it fixed. It's a timing problem or something like that," he said.

"I'm not sure what to do, George. I want to hug you and beat the crap out of you … or at least try too."

George said with a chuckle, "Well, unless you know a few new moves, Brent, you better just hug me. You always had trouble getting the best of me. You're lucky you had your driver's license and registration in order. I might have given you a harder time than all this!" They both smiled and then hugged. He gave Brent's driver's license, registration, and insurance card back. They were glad to see each other.

"Are you still mad at me for what I did to you and your lovely bride on your wedding night? It was a joke, George."

"Oh, I'm not mad at that. I actually forgot about it. I just felt it was my duty to give you this warm welcome!"

"Well, you're lucky I'm a forgiving man. For that stunt, George, you're buying me something to drink. There are a couple of restaurants down the road. So let's go." George nodded.

They got into their cars and drove down the road to one of the restaurants there. Of course, they were exceeding the speed limit, with George leading the way.

Brent started to think about his college days. George and he were very good friends. George helped him out a lot because Brent's parents didn't care about what happened to him. George knew Brent was on his own back in those days.

As George led the way to a restaurant, he thought to himself, *I never could understand how parents could be that way. I just can't believe parents could almost discard their child like an old pair of shoes. At least my parents weren't like that. But how did Brent learn to survive it? Maybe he hasn't and is just hiding it. One thing is for certain - it seems that he has done well for himself. He drives one of those German sports cars for cry in' out loud. I'm glad for him. He deserves it. Not too many people know him like I do, well, like I used to at least.*

Within a few minutes, they approached the business district of the town. They pulled into Bob's Fastlane restaurant. Brent got out of his car. There was a big smile on his face. He strutted over to his friend's unit, pulling up his trousers like a police officer does when he adjusts his holster after getting out of his unit.

They both chuckled a little. "Don't give up your day job. Acting isn't in the cards for you. Oh, one more thing. If you speed in my town like that again, I'll haul your sorry butt into our jail for the night." George said with a little attitude.

"Well, if you try to pull me over again, don't be

surprised if I don't do what you say, BUDDY! I don't know if you can catch me with that car of yours," Brent said jokingly.

George quickly retorted, "Maybe, but I know you can't outrun the radio." They both had a good laugh with that.

They went into the restaurant. Brent decided what to get to drink, and George decided what to get from the menu above the counter. After both orders were placed, Brent told the young kid behind the register, "This guy is picking up the tab..." George smiled and proceeded to pay.

"Will this be for here or to go?" the kid asked.

"For here," they said at the same time.

They got their food and drinks and found a table to sit at.

"Well, Brent, it looks like you have done well for yourself. I see your driving a BMW. When I left town, you were working for the city as an engineer, if I remember correctly."

"Things are going well. I'm into computers now. I have been for a long time." Brent stated.

"Why did you change your career path?"

"I didn't have the drive for the other anymore. I started to play around with computers a few years before that. I realized I had a natural knack for it."

"Good to hear. So how is Sue and your daughter doing?"

Brent looked down and paused for a few moments. He wondered how he should answer his friend. "My daughter died fifteen years ago this month. Sue died about ten years ago. My second daughter Carol just graduated from college with a degree in psychology. She completed her bachelor's degree in two and a half years. I'm not sure what drove her, but I'm proud of her."

George felt true sorrow for Brent. He looked down. *Brent just can't seem to shake some of this bad luck in his life. I had hoped he wouldn't have to endure more tragedy in his life. I don't know what to say to him.*

Brent continued. "After my daughter died, Sue and I had

so much trouble dealing with it. We sought counseling. Thankfully, we got with the right support group. It helped. However, it took many, many years just to get a handle on it. So many things happened after that tragedy that I never expected. Almost all our friends abandoned us. The others didn't visit or even call. I learned later that was normal because they saw how fragile life was and realized that the same thing could happen to them. And they didn't want to deal with it. Their nightmare is our reality. So basically our friends were gone. That was strange because when we needed them the most, they weren't there. Then there was this void in my life. My heart wept for her." Brent paused for a few moments.

"Somehow I managed to continue to work. But it was so difficult. Time seemed to stand still for many years. It took a long time for that to change."

George felt Brent's pain and anguish. He searched for any words to say that could comfort him. "I'm so sorry. I can't begin to imagine what that was like for you."

"You know, George, when you gave me your 'Welcome greeting', I had a flashback of her death in the hospital. I thought for sure I was going to see those pearly white gates and see her smiling face again. A part of me wasn't afraid to die because I would be with her."

George put his fork down and put his forehead on both of his hands. He just sat there and shook his head. *What did I do? I didn't have any idea that I could have caused such, such... Saying sorry doesn't even come close to expressing how I feel right now.*

"Brent, I am so terribly sorry for doing that to you. I feel like a jerk. Please forgive me."

Brent saw his old friend's anguish. He reached over and put his hand on George's shoulder. "Ah, it's ok. Of course you're forgiven. Don't worry about it. I just hope I paid the ultimate price so you won't have to.

George put his hands down on the table, still shaking his

head a little ... feeling like a complete idiot.

Brent took a few sips of his drink and continued. "So, enough of this stuff. What's been going on with you over all these years we've been out of touch? Are you still that meat and potatoes eating guy? Oh, are you still married to that lovely lady? How long have you been married now? Isn't it like fifty years or so?" Brent asked in a joking manner.

Choosing his words carefully, George responded, "You think you are a funny man, don't you? Yes, I'm still a meat and potato's guy. Let's see, June and I have been married for twenty-two years last month, NOT fifty. We have three children. Two are in college and one is a senior in high school. I'm thankful for financial aid."

"Well, as I remember your wife, she was a great lady! I can't believe she is still putting up with you. What did she see in you anyway?" Brent said sarcastically with a Cheshire cat smile.

George just grinned because he knew Brent didn't mean any of the sarcasm.

"I guess you have had some fun making those three kids!" he said with a devilish grin on his face. "Well, that's great. You look happy too. And it looks like you still work out!"

They continued talking and filling in some of the gaps since they last saw each other. It seemed like they picked up right where they left off many years ago. It was as if they were still brothers.

"So, why are you out this way, Brent?"

"Well, George, it's like this..." Brent told him about Grace.

"Interesting. Do you think anything might come out of it?" George responded.

"Oh, I don't know, George. I'll see what happens!"

The minutes turned into an hour. They got up and left the restaurant as they continued to talk. Outside, George's radio interrupted their conversation. The dispatcher started talking and George picked up the mike, acknowledging the call.

As George turned to him, Brent asked, "Anything dangerous?"

"Maybe. It's a domestic with a possible gun involved."

They walked to George's unit. They hugged and George said sincerely, "Well, it was good to see you after all these years, buddy. Here are my phone numbers, Brent. Give me a call sometime and we'll catch up on things. I'd like you to see June again. And if the kids are home, I'd like you to meet them! I'd like to talk more right now, but duty calls. Try to stay out of trouble. And, watch your speed." George said with a smile."

"Same here, George. And as for the speed thing, we'll see..."

They got into their cars. George backed out quickly, gave Brent a wave, and headed out of the parking lot. He turned on his flashing red lights and siren. Soon his squad car disappeared into the darkened streets.

Brent pulled out of the parking lot and headed for home. Brent reflected about his old college friend. *Gosh, he had a 4.0 grade-point average in college. If I remember correctly, his dad was an electrical engineer and had several patents on products that I saw in the market place years later. Hmmm, he never wanted any of his father's money either. I guess most people would think that is strange. He could have been almost anything he wanted in life. It makes me wonder why he chose to be a cop. Well, we need good law enforcement officers who know the law and how to enforce it!*

George headed towards the call he received. His lights were flashing and the sound of his squad car accelerated through the town streets so he could get there as soon as possible. Officers are somewhat fearful of any situation that may involve guns. They never know whether there is drinking and/or drugs involved because the perpetrator(s) or alleged perpetrator(s) are not thinking straight and are usually very difficult to deal with due to the emotions that can be involved.

George approached the address. It was a low-income area with some boarded-up houses. There were no working streetlights in the immediate area. He saw one of his fellow officers pulling up at the same time from the other end of the street. He turned off his flashing lights. They both stopped very near to the house and parked their cars. The road was a narrow, one-lane street, with allowed on one side of the street. No overnight parking on the street.

Both officers got out of their cars, being observant of the surrounding homes. He saw his buddy Stan Day's unit. He was an 18-year veteran of the force.

The wind was blowing now. Papers and debris were rolling down the street. It gave an eerie feeling, like something out of a Halloween movie. The house was surrounding by a four-foot high white fence (its paint was peeling) that ran along the whole length of the sidewalk.

They approached the ranch-style house, which had white aluminum siding and black shutters. The porch didn't have any windows or screens in it. The porch light, which was just over the door and centered in the ceiling, was on. There was a big picture window on the right side of the house and a matching window on the left. The door was in the middle. The lights were on in both windows. The front door was open and the screen door was closed. The hallway inside the door was dark.

"Hey, Stan, I don't see anyone inside. Do you?" George said in a hushed voice.

"No." Stan answered.

"I'll knock on the door." George said rather quickly.

Stan nodded as they both walked up the walkway in front of the house. George slowly walked up the three steps onto the front porch. He looked inside the screen door to see if there was any activity. The main door behind the screen door was wide open. Stan stayed on the first step.

George approached the door and paused, listening for any sounds inside the house. He then knocked, while looking around, and said, "This is the police…" Both Stan and George had their hands on their service revolvers.

They waited for a response. There was none. George knocked again and said in a louder voice, "This is the police…"

"Come on in," a female voice responded.

They looked at each other for a moment. The hallway light came on. George opened the door and went through it rather cautiously with his hand still on his weapon. Stan walked up the stairs onto the porch. He grabbed the door that George just walked through and held it open.

A young lady was walking down the hallway towards them. She was around five foot six, red hair, muscular build, wearing shorts and a tight t-shirt with bare feet. She approached the door. The floor made a slight creaking noise with every other step she took.

George started by saying, "Hello ma'am. We got a call that there was a domestic disturbance here and a gun might be involved. Who else is in the house?"

"My husband, but I don't know where he is."

"I'm over here in the kitchen." A voice was heard.

Both officers looked at each other. George asked the woman to step outside.

Stan and George drew their service revolvers and held them pointed at the floor. Then Stan began talking to the husband.

"Sir, slowly come out of the kitchen and come to the front door. I want to see your hands first."

"Ok. No problem." He shouted from the kitchen.

They could hear the legs of the chair screech across the floor as if he was getting up. Soon, a pair of hands slowly appeared from around the corner, then arms and soon, he was standing right there at the corner. The man was about five foot three, with blonde hair and around 160 pounds. He slowly walked towards the front door.

Stan continued, "Step over here by the door, sir, and put your hands on the wall and spread your legs for me. You are not under arrest at this moment. We just want to make sure you're not carrying a weapon. Do you have a gun or anything else we should know about?"

The man did as he was told adding,

"No. I don't have any weapons on me, officer."

Stan frisked him anyway. Stan went through his pockets, but only found a wallet, a lighter, and a key ring full of keys. Stan handed them to George.

"Ok. Is there anyone else in the house?" Stan asked nervously.

"No. Not that I'm aware of … other than my wife."

"Do you have any guns in the house right now?" Stan continued.

"Yes, we do. It's upstairs locked up in the bedroom," the man stated while his hands were still on the wall.

"Do you have a license to possess that firearm?" George asked.

"Yes, I do. The license is in my wallet."

"Pull it out for me, sir."

The man turned to look at the officers and took his wallet from George. He found his permit in the wallet and handed it to Stan. It matched the address of the house. It was a pink form. Everything on the slip of paper checked out properly.

"Ok. Stay right here." Stan instructed the man.

George escorted the woman off the front porch and walked down the steps with her. "Ok, ma'am, what happened here tonight? Were you the one that called the police?"

"Yes. Me and my husband were having a heated argument, and it got out of hand. He got really mad because I was holding a frying pan and threatened to hit him with it. I'm bigger and stronger than he is. So he said if I didn't put it down, he would have to get the gun. Well…"

She paused trying to keep her voice from cracking and the tears from flowing so George could understand what she was trying to tell him.

"Well, you see, he lost his job today, and we don't have much money left. He went out and spent some of the money from his last paycheck on beer instead of food. I guess I started to lose it a little and really wanted to whack him on the head with a frying pan. I started for him, and he took off for the bedroom where we keep the gun. I got scared and called the police."

"Did you hit him with the pan?" George asked.

"No," she said.

"Did your husband get the gun? Did you see it?" he continued.

"I don't know if he got it or not. I didn't see a gun. After I called the police, I went and hid in the closet in the hallway. And that's where I stayed until you two came."

George stated, "Wait here. I'll be right back."

While George was talking to the wife, Stan was gathering information from the husband. Stan asked, "What's your version of what happened here tonight, sir?"

"My wife got upset when I spent some of my last paycheck unwisely. She picked up a frying pan and threatened to knock me on the head with it. I went to the bedroom and locked the door just in case she decided to come upstairs with it. After a few minutes, I didn't hear anything so I went back to the kitchen and to see if she had cooled off. When I saw she wasn't there, I sat down at the table. I sat there thinking about things. Then I heard what I thought were voices, and I heard her walking around and talking to you two."

"Wait right here, sir."

George walked up the stairs and entered the house again. Both officers stepped into the living room to discuss what action, if any, needed to be taken.

"Ok, George. Looks like things have settled down here.

But we need to confiscate that gun. We don't have a warrant, but if the husband leaves, I think we can get the wife to give it to us."

"Let's do it, Stan."

Stan and George asked the husband to go out on the front porch so they could talk with both of them.

"Well, at this point, no law has been broken that we can tell. There are no signs of violence and no physical marks on either of you. Do either of you want to file any charges at this time?" George asked.

They both said almost at the same time, "No."

Stan continued, "Ok then. I guess there is no reason for us to stick around at this point. Do you have a friends or family member's house that you can to go and stay for the night, sir? The emotions are a little high at the moment between you and your wife. We just want to make sure that we don't get called back here tonight, because if we do, someone will be going to jail."

"Yes, I do," he said. The man went back into the house to call for a ride and gather some personal items. George went with him. Shortly thereafter, they came out with a bag. The man walked down the stairs and down the block.

George told Stan, "He called a friend to pick him up. He's been drinking, so we don't want him driving."

"Are you going to be ok here tonight, ma'am?" Stan asked.

"Yes. I believe so. All this is probably more my fault than his. I shouldn't have done it, you know, threaten to go after him with the frying pan," she said with a guilty conscience.

"Well, people usually don't like it when someone is coming at them with a frying pan with the intentions of harming them. You seem like a nice couple. Maybe tomorrow after you both would have had time to cool down, you can talk this out." Stan added. She nodded.

"He's a good man. I get too aggressive sometimes …

and short tempered. It doesn't last long though…"

"Now we need to see the gun, ma'am. Where is it?" Stan asked.

"Why do you want to see it? My husband has a license to possess and carry it." the wife asked.

Stan continued, "We are going to confiscate it just in case he comes back home angry. We don't want either of you to have access to it, just in case someone is, shall I say, not themselves."

The wife hesitated, but then decided to give them the gun.

"Ok. I'll bring it down."

"I'll go with you. Tell me where it is, and I will go with you," Stan stated firmly.

They both went upstairs. She told him where the gun was, and Stan asked her to stand back. She stood back as he picked up the revolver and emptied out the rounds. They went back downstairs with Stan holding the gun.

The officers left the house and stood at the curb waiting for the husband's ride to appear. Neither one said a word. Within a few minutes, a car arrived. The husband walked over and got in. The car turned around and headed down the street and out of sight. After a few moments, George noticed Stan had a blank stare on his face.

"Hey, Stan…"

Stan didn't say anything or acknowledge his fellow officer and friend.

"Hey, Stan. Earth to Stan. Can you hear me?" he said in a jokingly manner.

Stan blinked his eyes, shook his head and turned to his buddy. "Yeah, George."

"What's going on, buddy? It seems like you are staring into space. What's on your mind?"

"I don't know. I was just thinking a little. It appears this couple has a decent relationship. It seems like stress just got the best of them tonight. I find myself wondering why my wife and I can't have a good relationship and talk about our problems and concerns to get them resolved."

"Are you and your wife having problems again?" George asked in an apprehensive voice.

Stan just shrugged his shoulders and didn't say anything.

"Are you ok, Stan?"

"Yeah. I was just thinking and wishing a little. I'll talk to you later, George."

With that, Stan got into his unit and took off. George stood there for a few moments trying to figure everything out. Finally, he shook his head. He got into his unit and left the scene.

Chapter 4

The next morning, the sun was shining brightly. There was not a cloud in the sky. Brent was still fast asleep. He was awakened by the sound of his front door opening. Then he heard a sweet female voice calling out something. He slowly arose from bed, put on his bathrobe and made his way through the bedroom door and into the hallway. He continued down the hallway to where he could hear the very chipper voice coming closer.

Brent, half-awake, heard the female voice again as he got closer to where he thought the voice was coming from.

"Hi, Dad!"

"Oh. Hi, Carol." Brent said in relief with a yawn.

"I woke you up, didn't I? I'm sorry. You know it's almost 10 am?"

"Oh, really? It doesn't matter. Oh, by the way, good morning. What brings you over, young lady?" he said trying to wake up and wiping his eyes.

"Oh, I just wanted to stop by and say 'hi.' I haven't seen you for a couple of weeks. How are things going? By the way, I started my new job last week. It's great. I really love it. I'm starting at the bottom, but I have the chance to move up in the organization."

"Yeah? Well, move up in our family organization by giving me a hug."

They gave each other a big hug. They walked to the kitchen as she continued talking about her new position with a lot of excitement. They sat down at the breakfast nook.

"So, it sounds like they are treating you well. That's great. You deserve it. Your mother would be proud of you."

"Yeah, I sort of felt her presence there. It was a little strange I guess too." Silence filled the air.

"Are you ready for breakfast or are you going to work out first Dad?"

"I'll have breakfast first, I guess. Why? Are you hungry too?"

Carol answered, "Yes, I am. How about I make it? You made breakfast most of the time, so let me treat you. Do you remember when we had our breakfasts together? It was great, some very nice memories too. So what'll you have, Dad? Do you want the usual three eggs, English muffin and a grapefruit?"

"That sounds just great!" Brent said with a smile. She started to make breakfast. He got up and went to the sink to get a drink of water.

"So, Carol, how is David doing? Are you still seeing him?"

She glanced up a bit and slowly started to answer. "Well, we are taking a break right now. He's ok. But I'm beginning to think he is not my type. I'm only 21, just out of college and have a lot to do and enjoy before I get really seriously involved with someone. I'm just trying to have some fun. The strange thing is, a lot of guys just want one thing. I'm sure you know what I'm talking about. You were the one that told me all about that so many times," as she gave a glancing look.

Brent just smiled. "Well, I'm really proud of you, Carol.

I see you really understood what I tried to explain to you. I'm glad that you are able to put it together like you do. One thing is for sure - most people don't learn from history. When they don't, they are doomed to repeat the same mistakes as those that have gone before. And that's sad."

"So, Dad, sunny-side up or scrambled? Or should I say confused as you called it?"

"How are you cooking yours?"

"Mine are scrambled. But I'll do yours differently if you want."

"No, that's ok, Carol. Confused will be just great!"

They both smiled and stood there for a few moments without saying a word. The muffins and sliced grapefruit were done about the same time as the eggs. Then they both sat down and started eating. Before they knew it, the food was all gone.

"I guess we were both hungry this morning. We packed that away rather quickly," she said.

Then there was silence. Carol slowly pushed the plate away from her a bit and started talking in a somber tone.

"I don't say this often enough, Dad, but I really appreciate what you did for me while I was growing up. I know it was tough on you. You sacrificed a lot so I could get as good a start as possible in life. I'll never forget that either. I just wanted you to know that."

"Honey, if I had it to do over again, I wouldn't change a thing. You are worth it. You got a really good dose of what life was all about at an early age."

She looked down briefly, nodded her head in acknowledgement and said, "Yeah, but I understand more about what is important in life." The closeness they felt towards each other was very rare indeed.

"So, how do you like living with Pam? It must be nice to live so close to work," he said.

"It's kind of exciting! Pam is just the same-old Pam as she was in high school - unpredictable and nuts."

"Good. I'm happy it's working out for you. On another subject, I want to talk with you about something, ok?"

"Sure, Dad, go for it!"

"Why did you cram four years of college into two and a half? I mean, I'm proud of you for your accomplishment and graduating. But I always wondered why you pushed yourself so hard."

She didn't say anything for some time, but Brent waited patiently. He knew she would answer when she was ready.

"Dad, we are so much alike. I was going to bring this up, because I wanted you to know. Recently, I began to analyse some of the things I have done and why. The first thing I realized is that I drove myself hard so that you would notice me and my accomplishments. I was having an imaginary competition, constantly feeling inadequate to receive the same unconditional love you had given my sister who died and went to be with our Lord. I guess I wanted the love you reserved for her. I felt you idolized her. I mean, I never knew her because she died before I was born."

Brent's mouth dropped open in shock. He started to speak, but she stopped him by raising her hand.

"Dad, let me continue please. This was my own inner war. I know you did the very best job you could have done with the knowledge and wisdom you had at the time. Mourning the loss of my sister for so long negatively affected me in many ways. As a teenager, I didn't understand. Even with the counselor's help, I couldn't completely put into words how I was feeling because I really didn't know. I learned so much about myself in college, which has helped me truly heal as best as I probably will. I also see that you didn't love me any less than you did her. I just misinterpreted your actions at times."

Brent said thoughtfully, "Wow. I know many times brothers and sisters compete for various reasons, you know, sibling rivalry, but I didn't put two and two together. I wish I knew sooner. I might have been able to do something or…"

Carol spoke up interrupting Brent. "Wait, Dad, how could you have known? I didn't even know. I needed to figure this out on my own ... to carve out my own path in life. There was nothing for you to help me with. I had to see it and figure it out on my own. It's all part of growing up. You gave me the solid foundation to work with. It's up to me to do the rest of it."

Brent looked down for a moment. Then she perked up with some positive energy.

"Say, Dad, on another subject, when are you going to get out and start seeing someone special? Just as you are concerned for my happiness, I in turn am concerned for yours! It's been a while and you're not getting any younger - better looking and smarter maybe, but not the spring chicken you used to be," she stated with her wonderful smile.

He was a little taken back by the question, but nevertheless did appreciate the spirit that was behind the words. They could talk about almost anything. They respected each other's thoughts and feelings.

"You are your father's daughter. That's for sure. That's something I would say to someone if I felt it was needed. Well, to answer your question with the same directness, I have a special friend I might be meeting in about two weeks. Someone I knew many years ago. I'm actually looking forward to seeing and talking with her again. Do you remember Grace? She attended our support group meetings."

Carol looked slightly surprised and grinned a little as she searched for the proper words to say. "I don't recall you mentioning her at all in the past. So you think this is serious between you two?"

"Serious? Oh I don't know. She is coming here for the weekend and we'll have some fun. Then we'll see what happens between us. It's so strange, Carol, but we have this connection, this attraction, or chemistry, like it's subconscious. I'm not sure which one or maybe all the above. But while I'm excited about it, I'm taking it just one step at a time. We're just going to have some fun and catch up on things." Brent said with a hopeful attitude.

"Well, you know I'll have to meet her sometime. I want to see if this lady is good enough for my dad. Not that it would make a big difference." She said with some firmness.

"Oh, look at the time. I got to run, dad. Thank you for breakfast." She arose from her seat, put the dishes in the sink and hugged her dad. "If I don't leave now, I'll be late for a dentist appointment. I love you. Bye."

"What's the matter with your teeth," he asked.

"Dad, I'm just going to the dentist to have my teeth cleaned."

"Oh, ok. I love you too! Drive safely."

"I will, dad. I won't peel out leaving rubber on your driveway this time…"

With that they hugged again and she left. Brent closed the front outside door and looked out the window as Carol started her car and pulled out of the driveway. She waved good-bye to him as she drove off. He waved back. He started to remember the teenage years they both endured as she grew up.

The days passed rather quickly. Grace and Brent continued to talk back and forth through email. They continued to grow a little closer together.

The evening before she was scheduled to arrive, they had a very lengthy conversation on the phone. *I haven't heard her voice for over ten years. What a beautiful voice it is too - full of energy and excitement. She hasn't changed much since I last spoke with her.*

Long after the conversation ended, Brent's thoughts were wandering down memory lane. He felt the anticipation of seeing her building up again. His stomach felt like it was full of butterflies. He just wanted the next day to come as quickly as possible. He eventually forced himself to go to sleep. After tossing and turning for most of the night, he somehow fell asleep.

When the alarm went off at his normal waking up time, he jumped out of bed with joy saying, "Yeeeeesssssss!!"

He took a deep breath and began his normal morning routine. He stood in front of the mirror brushing his teeth a little bit longer than usual. He also checked his breath a couple of times. He looked into the mirror, smiled and said, "That's just right!!" He couldn't wait to leave for work.

He had trouble focusing on his work that day. He was a little nervous for many reasons. *I wonder whether she will come. Think positive now. Wait ... don't think. Just enjoy the moment for what it is. There may never be another one like it. But then, you never know what will happen ... as she would put it.*

Chapter 5

In another city, in another state, a car pulled up to a parking spot. It was a beautiful day with the sun shining, and the sound of birds' chirping could be heard all around. A lady got out of her car in a hurry with a briefcase and a cup of coffee. The sound of leather heels could be heard as she walked purposefully towards the employee entrance of a five-story commercial building.

The building was round with an outside facade that was almost all-reflective glass. It reflected all the trees, flowers, the sun, and the clouds that passed overhead. She walked up and put in her code into the keypad with the cup of coffee still in her other hand. When she heard the clicking noise, she pulled the door open and walked in.

She walked along the light-gray marble floor to the elevator. The sound of water running could be heard throughout the foyer area of the main floor. There was a magnificent waterfall in the middle of the lobby. All the products that the company marketed were in the center of the waterfall. The structure was all metal with a medium grey color. She had seen this waterfall many times, but today it seemed to have a different meaning than it had in the past. She pushed the 'up' button and waited for the elevator. A man approached the elevator. They said 'good morning' to each other and looked towards the elevator waiting for it to open. It soon did, and they both got in. He pressed button '3', and she pressed button '5'. As the elevator started its ascent, the man looked at his watch. When the elevator stopped at the third floor, the door opened and the man got out. The door closed, and she continued her ride until it stopped on the fifth floor, where she got off. She said 'good morning' to the receptionist and continued to her office.

Her office was decorated with dark-colored, cherry-berry wood furnishings. There were two chairs in front of her desk, which was on the left side of the room. The design of the chairs matched the executive chair behind her desk, but they were smaller in size. She walked around the desk and put her briefcase down on the floor. She sat down in the chair and looked at some of the papers that were scattered all over her desk. She took another sip of coffee and noticed she had some phone messages. She checked the messages. One of them was a customer with a complaint. She jotted down some notes and hung up.

The phone rang. Grace answered it and heard Sally, one of the customer service reps, explain Mr. Wright's missing weeble problem. Grace started to snicker with a huge grin on her face. "Thanks, Sally. Put him through…"

"Good morning, Mr. Wright. My name is Grace Wyne. I'm the customer service supervisor. How can I help you?"

In an irate tone, Mr. Wright yelled,

"I'm at the end of my rope. I've tried to be patient for two weeks now. I've been waiting for my missing weebles. I spoke to one of your customer service reps a week ago. She assured me that my order would be sent overnight. Three days later, I still didn't receive my weebles; thereby prompting me to call customer service again. The customer-service rep said she didn't understand the problem, confirmed my address, and said it would be taken care of immediately. I waited through the weekend, and on Tuesday, I called your 'great customer service department' again. The customer-service rep stated the order was shipped, but noticed that notes were made on the order. They told me something about some college kids hijacked the delivery truck that contained my order. She apologized profusely and said it would be taken care of. Obviously, I haven't received my weebles yet, or I wouldn't be talking to you. I sell a lot of these weebles as you can tell by the size of my orders. So tell me, 'Ms. Wyne, what is the probability of me receiving my weebles in this lifetime?"

While Grace was listening to Mr. Wright, she looked up his account on the computer and found that everything he was saying had been entered into the history. Grace exhaled and, in the most professional, serious tone she could muster, said, "Mr. Wright, prepare yourself for what I'm about to say. I'm truly sorry for all the inconvenience you have been through. I see here in the computer that you're a longstanding customer, and you pay your account on time. I've also read the history of the problems with your recent order. That includes all the phone calls you have made in an attempt to get your weebles. There is nothing to say at this point because actions speak louder than words. I'm going to personally run over to the warehouse and have them courier your order to the airport for same-day shipping. You will have your weebles today by 5:00."

"I've heard this before. This is starting to sound like a broken record. What else are you going to do for me? I'm a good customer, I pay on time, and I'm tired of all this talk and no weebles..."

Grace took a deep breath and tried to maintain her composer as she spoke, "We will credit your account..."

"That's all?" he said. "That's the best you can do? Throw a few bucks at me and it's enough to compensate me for not having my weebles? Look at all the sales I'm losing right now?"

Grace calmly responded, "I'm sorry you feel that way, sir. What else can we do to make this situation satisfactory for you?"

"Well, you can start by sending me two more cases of weebles at no charge, TODAY."

Grace, who was getting tired of this conversation, but remembering her role, responded, "I don't believe this will be a problem. I will call you back within the hour to confirm that three orders of weebles will be shipped today. I'm showing they are in stock."

Mr. Wright paused and then answered back rather gruffly, "We'll see. The proof is in the pudding..."

With that last comment, he hung up. Grace put down the phone shaking her head. She grabbed a small piece of paper and saw her friend Beth standing in the doorway.

Grace asked in an elevated tone, "How long have you been standing there?"

"Since the part where you said 'I'm sorry you feel that way, sir...'"

Grace entered the order into the computer. Then she started writing some words on a small piece of paper. Beth was a little puzzled at what she was writing. She walked over to a chair and sat down.

"What are you writing, Grace?" Beth asked.

Grace held up one-finger briefly, signaling her to wait, which Beth did. Grace finally put down her pen, took the piece of paper and put it in her shoe. She proceeded to get up and walk around her office for about a minute.

Beth was surprised by what she saw and asked, "Mind telling me what this is all about?"

Grace smiled rather intensely and said, "Do you remember the seminar I took last month on handling difficult customers? Well, this technique comes from an ancient Chinese secret."

"Oh, really?"

"No, not really. I just made that part up. But it is a great stress reliever," Grace said with her witty smile.

Beth got up and closed the door. She then sat back down (leaning forward onto the desk) and said in a joking manner, "Ok, the coast is clear. What is this ancient secret?"

"When you have a 'difficult' customer who starts to irritate you, you take their name, write it on a piece of paper, and place it in your shoe. Then you walk around on it, pretending it is that person."

"Does it work?"

"It actually does, very well in fact." Grace added. Then they both broke out in a fit of laughter.

After the laughter died down, Beth asked, "I can't imagine he dampened your day too much. Aren't you leaving about 1:00 or so?"

"Well, it did dampen it for a few brief moments, but that has passed now. And, yes, I'm leaving about 1:00. That's four hours and 32 minutes from now - that's if I was keeping track of the time." Grace then turned and glanced at the luggage that was behind her near the window.

At that particular moment, a cloud passed by that window so the sun shone its bright yellowish, orange rays onto the luggage on the floor. She had packed them the day before and brought them to work with her so she could leave for the airport directly from work to catch her flight.

Beth looked at the clock, amazed that Grace knew the exact time without ever looking at the clock.

"I guess I'm a little nervous about the trip. So what's going on? Are you just loitering around or do you need something to do?" Grace said jokingly.

"I'm just being nosey, Grace. I wanted to know how you are feeling and what's going on. I also wanted to tell you I'm really happy for you."

"Well, thanks. I'm not sure which emotion is the strongest right now. However, I'm feeling them all."

Grace started to fidget around in a slightly nervous

fashion. Beth started to say something but instead held her comments and observed Grace's actions.

Grace continued, "Let's see, let's print out this order and get it to the warehouse so it can be shipped this morning."

"I see you are busy, Grace, so I'll leave you alone to your work. Do you need a ride to the airport this afternoon?"

"No, I have that covered. Thanks anyway," as she continued looking at her computer screen.

Beth got up and started to leave her office, but stopped and waited for Grace to go to the warehouse. Grace went to the printer to grab the order and took it with her as she started to leave her office. She stopped and started to look around again on her desk. She looked under the papers, around the phone, and under the desk.

She stated, "It's around here somewhere…"

Beth walked over to Grace's purse. On the outside of it was a swipe card used to get into the shipping area. "Are you looking for this?" Beth asked.

Grace sighed a big sigh and said, "Thanks."

"Do you want some company on your trek to the warehouse? Beth asked.

"Well, I'm kind of…." Grace started to answer.

"Good. I don't mind going with you. Thanks." Beth said interrupting Grace.

Grace looked a little puzzled.

"Grace, I'm not done being nosey…" Beth said with a smile. She continued, "Ok, yes, I am being nosey. Tell me how you are feeling. I want to know, please. You seem a little gruff and very nervous."

"I guess my mind is preoccupied with seeing Brent tonight. It's been over ten years since I've seen him. He seems like he's the same guy I knew before, especially after we talked last night. I'm wondering if he's still the same person I knew way back then. A part of me is a little nervous about it. But another part of me wants to find out. I'm thinking I can go and if it doesn't work I can come right back. A lot of things are going through my mind. What do I do if I have a great time? We live so far apart. What if he turns out to be my soul mate ... the person I've been longing to meet for so long... I mean, I was thinking, do I REALLY want to be alone for the rest of my life?"

Beth listened intently. She was her friend and wanted the best for Grace. There was silence for a while as they walked. She wanted to ask her for more about Brent, but didn't. "Grace, I'm not going to tell you what to do. However, I will say this. If you feel that he is worth it, then go for it. I hope this is going to be a great time for you. I can almost feel that from you. You know, as we both say, you just never know what can happen! Hey, does he have a lot of money?"

"What? I don't know or care. What a question to ask."

They continued to walk through the door to the shipping area after she swiped her card on the keypad. She looked around and found Sam, the shipping manager, and said,

"Sam, can you do something for me? This order MUST go out this morning. We need someone to take it to the airport so it can be delivered to Mr. Wright by 5:00 this afternoon at his place of business. He buys almost a million dollars worth of products from us each year. What else do you need from me to make this happen?"

"Nothing. I'll make it happen," Sam said. "I'll get someone to pull the inventory right now and package it so that we can get it to the airport. I'll call a courier at the other end so they can deliver it today. On second thought, I'll run it to the airport myself."

"Thanks, Sam. I appreciate it! I'll call Mr. Wright and let him know what we're doing." Grace and Beth turned and walked back to Grace's office.

Beth started again. "Ok, now that that is out of the way, when are you coming back?"

"Sunday evening."

"Do you need me to pick you up from the airport? I mean, I have to know what happened. You know, I need to hear all the 'delicious' details," Beth stated with a smile.

"Thanks for the offer Beth, but I have that covered. Now I need to get back to work because I have four hours and two minutes before I need to leave."

"How do you do that, Grace? The time thing?"

Beth looked at her watch and shook her head.

Grace couldn't help but let out a smile.

"Ok, Grace, let me know what happens. Call me Sunday night when you get back."

Grace chuckled. "Ok, Beth!"

It was noon and Brent was heading to the company cafeteria for lunch. Half his day was over, and all that filled his mind was Grace's visit. He entered the cafeteria and stood in the line that led to the salad bar. While he waited in line, he made small talk with other employees. His friend Dave showed up to order lunch and got in the other line. Dave was hired around the same time Brent was years ago. They developed a friendship over the years. They worked in the same department.

"Hey, Brent. Are you ready to start your losing streak today? I mean, you might win most of the time, but today I think I just might be able to start my own winning streak!"

Brent just grinned and said, "You can try to hex me, but we'll just see what it does to the pieces!" (Brent won most of the time when they played chess. It always frustrated Dave because he hated to lose. But it was always fun, and he enjoyed playing against Brent. During their chess games, they would talk about the things that were going on in their lives.

"See you in room 614. Accounting is using the other conference room for a meeting," Dave said.

Brent nodded while paying for his lunch.

They met on the sixth floor in the conference room and sat down at the oval-shaped table. They set up the pieces and started the time clock.

They played and ate at the same time. Brent started

losing some pieces rather quickly, and Dave noticed that Brent wasn't reacting like he normally would when he lost pieces. Dave also noticed Brent had been checking his watch quite often, which he never did when they played. After a while, Dave stopped the game and looked at Brent.

Brent looked up at Dave and asked, "What? What? Why did you stop the game?"

Dave looked down briefly and said, "What's the matter? You're not yourself. Something must be bothering you. It seems like your mind is focused on something else. Am I right?"

Brent looked at his watch again.

Dave continued, "Ah, did you get a new watch? You've looked at it about six or seven times now in the past twenty minutes or so. Can I see it?"

"No, Dave. It's the same watch I always wear. But I might have a hot date tonight. I've got a lady who is flying in tonight. I'm going to the airport right after work today to pick her up!"

"Oh, really. That's cool. But what's this 'might' stuff? Do you think she's not coming? You did say 'might', correct?"

"Well, Dave, there's always a chance she won't make the flight, but after talking with her last night, she seemed to be excited about coming to see me."

"You haven't mentioned this lady to me before have you? So what's the story?" Dave asked and continued to eat his lunch.

"I knew her many years ago from the support group meetings we attended. You know, the support group that helped me to learn how to deal with the loss of my daughter," Brent said soberly.

"Yes, I remember you talking about that before." Dave paused, then continued. "If you don't mind me saying that's a strange place to meet someone. Did she help you in some way?"

Brent chuckled a little. "Yes, but I noticed some different things about her. She really seemed different. From the first time I met her, I noticed we seemed to click together. It was an attraction or a subconscious draw we had for each other. Of course, we didn't act on it because we were both married at the time."

"Wow. I bet that surprised you, huh? Did she tell you this or did you sense it?" Dave asked.

"I thought I saw it in her eyes. I sensed it." Brent said with a smile.

"Really now? What's her name and how long is she staying?" Dave sensed that this lady was important to Brent for many reasons.

"Her name is Grace, and she is leaving sometime Sunday." Brent smiled again.

"Well, Brent, I'm happy for you. I hope things work out for the best for you." Dave looked up on the wall and realized that their lunch hour was over.

"Well, you'll have to tell me what happens on Monday."

Dave started to put the chess pieces away. Brent looked at his watch and helped.

They went back to work. When Brent got back to his desk, he went online to check with the airline to make sure the flight was going to leave on time. It was.

A couple of hours later, Dave walked passed Brent's desk. Brent was checking his email.

Dave made a comment with a smile as he walked by, "Nice watch, Brent! Hopefully the faceplate won't wear off!" Brent just chuckled and smiled.

"You're funny, Dave. But don't give up your day job…"

Brent continued checking the time. The day seemed to take forever to end. The anticipation of Grace's arrival seemed to escalate his feelings and emotions, as it got closer to quitting time.

Finally, it was 5:00. He thought it would never come. *Let's see, she's due in at 6:10. That gives me plenty of time to get to the airport, park the car and patiently wait. Yeah, right, patiently wait. I'd better check to see if the flight is on time.* It was.

Brent got into his car and drove directly to the airport. He parked in the parking garage and set the car alarm. He made his way to the arrival terminals and checked the monitors. The flight was due to arrive on time.

He told her he'd be waiting for her by the baggage claim area. Because he didn't want to wait that long to see her, he walked over to the security area and waited there instead. Standing there leaning against a pillar for what seems like hours turned out to be only about 20 minutes.

Soon he saw a blonde lady walking out from the security area. Then he saw that smile, a smile that lit up the entire corridor. He knew her smile a mile away. Then he saw her blue eyes. *That's her all right.*

Oh, my gosh... look at her. Does she look good or what? He started to smile and his eyes lit up his entire face.

As she approached, they looked into each other's eyes and exchanged thoughts as if they had a telepathic connection. Then they embraced.

Oh my... can she hug or what...? The thoughts of her hug when they said good-bye many years ago after the meetings, came back like a flood. It seemed like the whole world was at peace now that they were together. They could sit together and simply talk or go out and do whatever. He closed his eyes ever so deeply as they embraced for many minutes. They didn't move an inch during that time. He opened his eyes and saw her long, beautiful golden-brown hair.

Oh my gosh, look at it. It's gorgeous. Brent couldn't help but think they were picking up right where they left off many years ago. That's pure friendship.

Finally, they decided it was time to get her luggage. So they started to walk down the corridor arm an arm.

"So, how was your flight? Where there any problems? Did they treat you all right?" Brent wanted to make sure their time together was special. His excitement was so escalated that he didn't wait for her to answer. Then he realized what he had just done...

"Sorry. I'm asking all these questions and not waiting for an answer..."

"I know. I feel the same way too. Everything was just great, Brent! But before we continue, let me look at you, at your face..."

She looked at him, directly into his eyes, all around his face. As she did, her smile got bigger and bigger.

"Just what I thought and felt. What a beautiful man you are!"

That comment sent Brent's heart in a flutter. Then she continued.

"Ok, I didn't have any trouble getting to the airport. But the flight seemed to last forever. But I'm here now. And it feels really great."

Brent agreed with her in his heart. *Wow, this feels so great. She is right! We never did this before. Oh my gosh, this feels so, so comfortable. We are like two peas in a pod. And look at her. She can't quit smiling. Of course, I can't either. It just seems like we are the only ones at the airport. There are other people, but we are not paying a bit of attention to them.*

He picked up her luggage and carried it to the parking garage. They tried talking to each other, but the excitement was so high that they could hardly talk as they made their way to his car. Both began to realize they were together. And the excitement and chemistry between them was so thick, you could cut it with a knife.

Then she saw his car. "Oh my, we are off to a good start here. That's my favorite color ... blue."

He smiled thanking God he had bought the blue car.

"Good. I'm glad. Then it'll be easier for you to drive it before you leave to go home." He said to her.

Though she didn't show it, she was thrilled by it. She never drove a BMW before.

"It's all part of the experience we'll have on your mini-vacation while you're here. Ok?"

She never said a word, but he felt the thrill she gave off with her emotions.

"Well, look at this. A personalized license plate, MY2NDBMW. That wouldn't stand for "My Second BMW" would it? Where is the first one?" She asked in an inquisitive voice?

They paused at the front of the car. Brent smiled and clicked the remote to disable his alarm. *She doesn't miss much.*

"The first one is in my garage. It's a convertible. I don't take it out when the wind is higher than ten mph because it might tarnish my baby's beautiful luster finish."

They looked at each other and laughed out loud.

He put the luggage in the trunk and went over to the passenger side of the car to open the door for her. After she was comfortable, he closed the door, hurried over to the driver's side and got in.

Wow! She's in the car with me. I can't believe it. What a thrill it is. She looks so lovely in it. I'm a little nervous about what to do next. Ok. Settle down. Start the car and get out of the parking garage.

The car roared to life and they left the garage. He paid for the parking and onto the highway they went. It was a seventy-degree night.

"Are you comfortable? We can open the moon roof to get some fresh air if you'd like."

"That sounds great. I got a little warm on the flight out here." She said.

"Go ahead and push that button right there." He pointed to the switch on the ceiling.

"Alright. You mean this one here? I don't want to start touching a bunch of buttons and suddenly I'm ejected from the seat," she said jokingly.

He was stunned for a moment. He started to laugh. He had no idea she was this funny. "Ah, don't worry about it. If it throws you out, then I'll come rescue you."

A big smile came pouring over her face. He had never seen that before either. That broke the ice. They both started to relax.

"This car is beautiful. It looks like it's brand new. I bet you have ladies interested in getting into it all the time. Are you fighting them off?"

There was another joke. He couldn't help but laugh out loud. She's a riot. This is going to be a great weekend.

"Well, not very often. I don't care to be involved with materialistic females like that. I don't care how beautiful the lady is."

"Well, I'm one of those materialistic girls, you know." She said sarcastically.

He knew she wasn't. *There's some more of her humor. This is great!!!*

It was so good to be able to talk to her again. It was medicine for a lonely soul.

He started the car and it roared to life. He pulled out of the garage and headed for the highway.

It warmed his heart so much to listen to her talk. Her fresh perspective on things was really refreshing. *Just like the old days.* As they drove down the highway towards the restaurant where they were going to eat, they talked about anything and everything that came up. Wherever the conversation went, they were happy to follow it where it led them.

There was a lull in the conversation as they were getting off the highway. He realized they were bonding, just like before. But this was different. It was more emotional and maybe part of it was spiritual, among other things ... maybe.

As they drove along the side roads, the conversation picked up again and he started to think, *I never felt this way about a lady before. We seem to have so much in common at this point.* They talked and listened to each other. *This is so fantastic!* They both thought. They respected each other's opinions whether they agreed or not.

Before he knew it, they were nearing the restaurant.

"Now, I have only one rule in my car. When there is a lady present, I have to open and close the door for her. Ok?"

When they arrived, he got out and opened her door.

"It's been a long time since anyone has made me feel important enough to open my door. You thought of everything didn't you?" she said rather humbly.

"Well, I hope I didn't miss any details concerning your stay. I want this to be a happy and memorable time for you, that is, if you don't mind."

"Well, I can check that one off!" she said.

He couldn't help but smile at not only what she said, but also at how she said it. There was a certain charm to her that just captured his heart and soul when she said things like that. It made his heart flutter.

"So what's going on here? Do you have a list of things you are looking for? If so, what's next to be checked off?" he said in a joking manner.

She looked at him and busted out laughing. He joined in her laughter. Then she gently stated, "You know, Brent, you need to be careful. I could get used to this very easily...!" He smiled at her. She grabbed his hand and held it as they walked into the restaurant.

He had never been to this restaurant before. He heard it was first class. He was told that if he wanted to show her a good time, he should take her here. He wasn't sure what to expect when they walked inside. They walked through the doors into the atrium and stopped where the hostess was standing. Just behind the hostess was a ceiling that had a breath-taking picturesque starry night sky that was softly lit up. The tables were surrounded by trees offering seclusion from the rest of the world. You could hear soft instrumental music and the murmur of people engaged in hushed conversation with candles lit on every table. They looked at each other. Neither one knew if this was the place they should eat at. It was a place for romantic couples to dine and enjoy each other's company in a quiet setting.

He asked Grace, "What do you think? Are you comfortable with this? We can go somewhere else if you wish."

She looked around, being taken back a little by all the beautiful decor and atmosphere inside. She didn't answer right away. She had to think about it. So he patiently waited for her to respond.

"Well, I'm not used to eating at places like this. Maybe we should check out another place."

Brent smiled at her charm. It was so refreshing to hear and feel it.

"No problem." He said. So they made their way out the door and walked down to a sports bar nearby. They got halfway through it when she stopped.

"You know, this place is somewhat noisy. I changed my mind. Let's try the other place. That's if it's ok with you." He looked in her eyes and smiled again. *She's courageous.*

"Let's go back then, Grace."

"That's fine with me," she said. So they turned around and walked back to the restaurant.

"Hello, folks. Did you change your minds?" the hostess asked courteously.

"Yes, we did," Grace spoke up. Brent just smiled.

She escorted them to a table off by themselves. It was a romantic room with about 20 tables. The setting was just right. The four-sided table picked for them was rather small, but had four chairs around it. The waiter came by and seated them, pulling out the chair for Grace as she sat down.

Brent pulled out the chair across from her and started to

sit down.

"Wait. Could you please sit over here next to me?" She flashed him a romantic look that melted his heart. He paused for a moment and wasn't able to think of anything to say.

"Of course. I would be delighted to sit next to a charming lady like you," he said softly.

Her smile got bigger and softer. Her eyes lit up the whole table, if not the entire room. His heart fluttered again at the gesture she gave him. It had been a long time since he had feelings like that. Actually, he couldn't remember when he had them last.

They looked into each other's eyes and enjoyed the moment. They weren't sure how long it would last.

"Well, this is a ..." he paused trying to find the words to describe it, "charming place. Are you sure you are comfortable here?"

She reached over and touched his arm gently and said, "Yes. This is just perfect. Are you ok with it?"

"As long as you are here, Grace, I'm fine with it too."

She brought out a different smile this time. "It's been so long since someone went to these lengths to make me feel this good. Thank you so much. We should be careful here. I could almost get used to this treatment." She chuckled a little. He could feel the appreciation in her voice.

"I'm only too happy to make it memorable for a lady of your stature." She took the compliment well, but was taken back a little by all the special attention she was getting. As far as he was concerned, that was ok.

"Well, let's see what's on the menu. Are you hungry or just starving?" Brent said with a little bit of humor.

"I'm not too hungry. I could probably eat half a cow, but nothing really big." He started to chuckle and laughed out loud. She continued,

"I have to warn you, I'm kind of like this a lot, my joking I mean. It just comes out. I'm like this at work too. I don't think you saw that part of me before."

"Oh, is that so?" he said acting surprised. "Well, I actually find it quite charming and entertaining. It might be something I could get used to very easily."

They looked at each other rather seriously and then busted out laughing again. They each knew what the other meant by the comments.

The rest of the evening went very well. As they started to catch up on the past, some tearful moments came out. They shared different things. At one point, she reached out to his hand to hold it while his tears flowed. At another point, he did the same for her. It was an evening they both would never forget. At one point in the evening, he began to realize that she didn't share her feelings much on very close personal matters. However, she wanted to hear his. That bothered him some. Plus, he wasn't used to someone caring for his thoughts and feelings like that. But he was patient and felt that maybe she would do the same down the road so he could understand her better. After the meal and dessert were over, they left the restaurant. It was a memorable time for them both.

They got into his car. It roared to life when he started it.

"We have a little drive ahead of us. Sorry I couldn't get a closer hotel."

"That's ok. How far is it?" He didn't answer, just smiled.

He left the parking lot and turned right. About forty feet down the road, a hotel entrance appeared. He turned right and pulled up to the front door.

"Wow, Brent, you're right. That was a long trip."

He turned to her and smiled. He opened her door and then got her luggage out of the trunk. They went inside to the check-in desk.

"Can I help you?"

"Yes, we have a reservation for tonight." Brent said.

"Great. What is the reservation number?" Brent gave the clerk all the information she needed.

"Will this be for both of you?" Brent turned to Grace

who just smiled.

"Just one … for tonight…" Graces right eyebrow went up, and she continued to smile.

"How will you be paying for this, sir?"

He pulled out his credit card and gave it to her. After the credit card information was taken and processed, he mentioned to the clerk, "Whatever this lady wants, make sure she gets it, ok? Well, unless she wants to buy the place. Then let me know on that!"

The clerk smiled back and said, "Of course."

"How many cards will you need, sir?"

"Just one," Brent stated quickly.

She coded the room card and gave it to him. They proceeded to her room. When they stepped into the elevator, he mentioned, "Now give me a call in the morning when you get up and about. There's no time frame so if you want to sleep in, that's fine with me. Ok?" She nodded.

He opened the door with the swipe card and made sure everything was just right with the accommodations. The room was very nice and comfortable. They walked in and he placed the room key on the table.

"Here's your coffee pot and different types of coffee. Is that ok?"

She nodded again.

He looked into the bathroom. "Are there enough towels for you?"

She looked in the bathroom and again nodded, but then looked down at the floor. Brent sensed something was wrong. He walked over to her and bent down, almost getting on the floor. He looked up into her face while she was looking at the floor. Her eyes were moist, and she was trying not to show her emotions to him at that point.

He smiled at her and asked, "Is this room not good enough? I can get you a different one if you want. If you don't like this hotel, there are two more that might be nicer than this one. But they are a little further away. I'll gladly take you there if you want."

She couldn't answer. All this was very overwhelming for her. She finally raised her head. He handed her a Kleenex to wipe her eyes. He thought about wiping them for her, but thought he'd save that for later, if there were a later.

"Do you want to talk about it?" She held up her right index finger as if to gesture for him to wait a minute. So he did.

As she stood there, he sat in one of the chairs ... patiently waiting for her to say what was on her mind. She came and sat down in the other chair. Soon she spoke, but in a broken voice because all the emotions that were coming out.

"I keep repeating myself here, but I can't ever remember when someone went to this much detail to make sure I was as comfortable as I could be. And this is only the first night."

She barely got all that out. She smiled and more tears flowed. He got another Kleenex and slowly approached her face with it. He paused to see if she was uncomfortable with him wiping the tears from her face. When she made no attempt to stop him, he wiped the tears from her beautiful eyes and cheeks. She tried to say thank you but couldn't. She was overwhelmed by his gentleness.

Who is this man? I've never seen anyone like him before. All the times we talked, I never realized he was so.... She couldn't put into thoughts what she was feeling.

Brent leaned over and gave her a hug. She hugged him back. She seemed to settle down. That was his cue to get up and leave so she could make her calls and or simply go to bed. But before he left, he squatted down about two feet away from her, because she was still looking down. Then he softly said to her, "You're welcome."

Her mouth dropped open a little. She was speechless. He got up and headed for the door. He opened it, turned and told her, "Sweet dreams." He left the room, closing the door behind him.

As he drove through the parking lot of the hotel, he stopped the car and looked towards her room. She had the curtains open and waved to him. He poked his hand through the open moon roof and waved back. Then he sped off onto the street and out of site. As he drove home, he could not believe all the fun he had being with her. *Could this be the start of something bigger between us? There can be no way I'm able to bond with someone like this ... and so quickly. It's too good to be true. There's got to be a catch somewhere.*

Then it dawned on him. *She's leaving the day-after tomorrow. I could be emotional for days or even weeks afterwards. Oh my gosh, what am I going to do about that? Well, we'll see how the rest of the time goes. Now try to get home safely so you can rest and enjoy the rest of the weekend with her. What a lady....*

Chapter 6

The next morning she called him from the hotel. "Good morning, Brent!"

"Good morning, Grace! Well, was everything ok? Did you sleep well or at least ok?"

"Yes. I slept just fine, thank you. I talked to my Mom last night to let her know I made it ok. I talked to her for about 30 minutes."

"Good. Did you tell her about last night? Was she pleased?"

"Oh, yes. I did update her on what happened. She was happy for me too!"

"Well, that's great. So are you ready for me to pick you up?"

"As a matter of fact, I should be ready when you arrive."

Brent said excitedly, "Great! I'll see you in a few minutes!"

Brent got into his car and picked her up at the hotel. They proceeded to get some breakfast and run around town.

They did some window shopping and stopped by a pizza place.

"Now, pizza, that's another one of those major food groups I was telling you about before!" He chuckled with a smile as she spoke.

"Good. Let's order and eat up," Brent said excitedly.

After they were done, they left the pizza house. It was a great day to be cruising around the area with the roof open. It was in the mid-70's and very pleasant with not a cloud in the sky. There were times they said nothing. Sometimes just being in the presence of a friend was enough. He sensed she had something on her mind. *If she wanted to talk, then she would have done so. I wonder if there is a problem that's making her so quiet. Just give her some space. If she wanted to share it, then she would have ... I think.*

After a long silence and just enjoying their time together, she spoke up.

"Now, that was really very nice. You can be a quiet companion. I can check that one off too," she said with a smile.

Brent asked, "Where is this list of things to check off? I'd like to see it if you don't mind. If I didn't know better, it feels a little like the Spanish Inquisition..."

Grace looked at him, but he couldn't hold a straight face. A grin crept over his face and he began to chuckle. Grace started to feel bad, but began to laugh herself.

They decided it was time to go to his house and chill for a while. She didn't see his home yet.

We'll enjoy a different type of emotional bonding now, I guess. Hey, just as long as she is near me, that's all that counts. This thought brought a smile to his face.

They pulled into his driveway. It was a white brick ranch-style house with black trim around the windows. It was beautiful to look at. Nothing flashy, but it spoke volumes because it had a touch of class to it. It had a three-car garage attached to it. He stopped the car outside the garage and they got out. The front door was black in color. He unlocked and opened it. They went in and she noticed the gray and white marble floor entrance.

"Wow, this looks like the same color of flooring we have in the atrium where I work, Brent."

"Is that a good thing?"

"Oh, yes. I like it."

It was nice and elegant, but homey too. The focal point was the fireplace, which you could see as you walked into the house. Off to the left was a living area - no TV there. It was mainly for entertaining or when you wanted to be away from the family room, which was off to the right side of the marble floor entrance. You had to take one step down to get into the family room. There was a huge flat screen high-definition TV with a DVD player and surround sound stereo speakers. Some workout equipment was in the room as well. He noticed her puzzlement with the exercise equipment being in that room.

"As you probably noticed, the reason why I keep my exercise equipment in here is so I can exercise while watching TV. Too many people forget or don't exercise because it's in a room by itself. So, right or wrong, that's why it's there."

"Well, that makes sense," she said.

He continued, "Thank you. Now over here is the kitchen. I picked the dark cherry-berry stained wood. As you will see, it's throughout the house. That kind of furniture has a nice touch to it. I thought I'd put it in the kitchen too so the house has a certain consistency to it. I went with the medium dark-blue marble countertop. I think it accents the whole room. Now over here is the dining area. As you might have noticed, it's also a morning room. We get the morning sun through these windows. It's very nice and warm. It helps start the day in a positive way!"

"Did I hear you say 'we'?" Grace asked.

"A figure of speech," Brent responded. "I see you are

listening. Thank you."

"I thought I had some competition for a moment," Grace said firmly.

"No competition, well at the moment ..." Brent said in a reassuring manner while grinning.

Then he turned around and they backtracked down the hallway.

"Down this hallway there are three bedrooms with three and a half bathrooms. Each bedroom has its own bathroom. The master bedroom has a hot tub and a big walk-in closet - big enough to hold clothes for the entire family. Or, a whole lot of women's shoes if need be." He chuckled, raised an eyebrow and smiled in her direction.

"Well, I guess I can check that one off too," she said while eyeing him.

He just shook his head and continued, "Of course, the bedroom is mostly blue in color. That's my favorite color. Some people think that color is a little too cold for a bedroom. But it's cooler in the summer and as for the wintertime, hey ... throw another blanket on if need be." He laughed as he said that.

"I like the bedroom color that's for sure. It makes me feel comfortable."

His eyes widened. "Well, I'm glad I picked these colors then? How comfortable does that make you feel, huh?? Was I just was thinking out loud there? Gentlemen don't talk that way."

She laughed and put her arm around his. She understood the humor and the innocence of it. So they walked arm in arm through the rest of the house as he described to her why this was this way and why that was over there.

"So, as you can tell, I designed this home myself. After I finished the basics of it on the computer, I took the file to an architect and let her finish up the plumbing, etc. for me. And this is pretty much the finished product."

"Well, I think it's great. It needs more blue for my taste,

but I like it. It has potential. It's classy too." She squeezed his hand gently. He squeezed her hand back a couple of times.

They went back through the house and towards a door in the kitchen. He opened it and stepped through. She followed him.

"Here is the garage. Here is my second sports car. It's a convertible. And blue, of course!!! This is another one of my fun cars. This one has more horsepower than the one we have been motoring around in. When I put the top down, it's just great. I was going to drive it today, but I decided to take the other one at the last minute. They were talking about rain, but it looks like it missed us. Do you like convertibles, Grace?"

"Yes, I do. The color is great too!"

"Now, let me take you to my favorite place ... my backyard."

They walked through the door at the back of the garage.

"You will notice that the floor is all concrete. There is a roof over half of the area. I have a mixture of flowers, shrubs, and two apple trees. My stainless steel grill is big enough to feed a lot of people. Now there's my two-seated glider along with a couple of other seats for visitors. I don't get too many visitors. The one side of the glider is empty most of the time. I get lonely sitting in it sometimes. Finally, look at that view of the lake... Now what do you think about that?"

"Wow... Look at that lake. And that white walkway I guess you would call it."

"I want to walk down that path with you later if you don't mind. But right now, I know someone who would love to sit in it with you..." pausing for a moment, while watching his facial expression she continued,

"As a matter of fact, she is impatiently waiting to sit there with you right now."

His eyes got a little wider at that moment. No woman ever said that to him before. It actually stunned him for a brief moment.

"Excuse me," Grace continued, "but how long are you

going to keep a lady waiting? She wants to try out the fit of this glider with you..."

After trying to clear his throat, "I beg your pardon. Please forgive me for being so, shall I say, insensitive to a 'lady's' needs."

That was enough talk. *This woman is incredible. I'm in trouble now. She knows my hot buttons. Oh, well.* He proceeded to sit down next to her.

"Ah, yes, this fits me just fine," she stated. "How does the glider feel now, with a lady in it by your side?"

He couldn't speak even though he tried to. She leaned over and looked into his eyes for a response. She saw the look in his eyes and just smiled. The look was enough. She cuddled up next to him and patiently waited for his answer. There was no hurry on her part. She was content to just sit there and take in the moment.

His thoughts drifted freely. *Two peas in a pod... I like the way all this feels. Gosh. It all feels so ... so comfortable, peaceful, and calm to me. And by the look in her eyes, I think she feels the same too. Oh my gosh, is this dream? If it is, then I don't want to wake up. Please let it be real...*

There was a nice breeze in the backyard. They could hear the bird's singing. They sat there and didn't say a word for a long while. She had her head leaned against his upper arm. She looked up into his eyes again. She liked what she saw. They just sat there and took in the moment together. Everything was right in the world now. They wondered if this was what harmony was like.

The afternoon turned into evening.

"Does your daughter know I was coming?" she asked.

"As a matter of fact, yes! She wanted to meet you. Maybe someday she will!"

As they continued to talk the time away, Brent asked. "Hey, are you hungry?"

"Now that you mention it, yes! I'm starting to hear either an earthquake or my stomach growling. And seeing that the furniture is not moving, it must be my stomach. What does the gentleman have in mind for this lady tonight?"

"How does Chinese sound? Do you like Chinese?" he asked.

"Sure do. Knowing you, I'm sure it's a great place."

"Then Chinese it is. It's one of my favorite places to go actually. This place is huge too." Brent said happily.

They got off the glider, went back to the car and took off for the restaurant. It was dusk now.

When they arrived at the restaurant, she noticed it was a buffet. The biggest one she ever saw. After indulging themselves, and almost creating a scene with all their laughter, they left. As they drove off, they started to talk about the restaurant and laughed about the experience.

"Did we just act like a couple of teenagers in there, Grace? I'm almost embarrassed by it. But after thinking about it, I'm not. If they didn't appreciate us being there and spreading good cheer, that's their loss."

Then he started speaking like he was acting in a play. They both busted out laughing. She made a few more jokes. He started to laugh so hard he almost had to stop the car because he couldn't keep it in the proper lane. He laughed so hard he cried. With all the tears in his eyes, he could barely see the road.

"Grab the wheel Grace or we're in trouble. I can't see the road through all the tears."

"Hey, do you think I'm a stunt driver here? I can barely see the road myself. Here, let me sit on your lap and drive that way. Will that help?"

There was silence for a brief moment and they busted out again into a bigger burst of laughter than before. Brent managed to get the car pulled over into a rest area before they had an accident. So they just sat there and cracked jokes for a while. They laughed so hard for so long their cheeks hurt. After the laughter settled down, they both looked up at the sky through the open roof. The lights from the rest area lit up parts of the interior of the car. It was a beautiful, star-filled sky with not a cloud in sight.

Brent spoke up. "We should have taken the convertible. I was worried about the wind. But we'll make due. We can recline the seats like this." The adjustments were on the right side of her seat next to the door, so he reached over her lap and adjusted her seat.

"How is that?"

"That's just fine. That's an interesting position you are in right now. Are you enjoying yourself?" she responded.

As he retracted his arm across her lap, he looked up into her face. She radiated a smile back at him, which made his heart race. He got back on his side of the car. Thoughts raced across his mind for a brief moment while he was in that position. Then Brent adjusted his seat all the way back.

He continued as he looked up. "Is that the big dipper over there? Where's the little dipper? There it is over there. Can you see it?" he asked her.

"Yes, I can! Hey, there's a satellite. And there's another one."

"Isn't that a plane over there?"

"I think so." She turned her head to him. He felt her look and turned to her. *Is she beautiful or what?*

"I'm having the time of my life, Brent. Thank you ever so much."

"Ditto for me!" he said while smiling and touching her face gently. She grabbed his hand and held it there for a while. Then they turned back to the stars.

"It's nice not to have any mosquitoes around here," he stated.

She just nodded. They sat there enjoying the night and holding hands.

There's nothing like building a relationship with the right lady. I had no idea it could be this fantastic.

They had no idea how long they just sat there looking up into the night sky holding hands. Finally, she repositioned her body so that she was on her side facing him.

"Have you ever considered getting involved with someone again? How many years has it been since Sue died? If that is too personal a question, then I'll understand if you don't want to answer it."

"No, that's ok. I'll answer it. I thought about it. There was no one whom I wanted to go out with that I thought wanted to go out with me. I was interested in one person, but I didn't think I was her type or I was right for her. She was a classy lady. Anyway, I just don't date. I guess I'm too picky. I don't want to go out just to go out and have a good time. Maybe that's wrong. I don't know. I'm a sensitive guy and sometimes women say things that really bother me. Many of them are hung up on a lot of personal issues and don't want to move on. They don't want to let go of them for whatever reason. Of course, I have my personal issues too. So who am I to say anything to anyone? So to spare myself the drama, I don't go out much."

He sensed that her emotions went down a notch as she looked away. It started to fill the air in the car. He slowly raised his hand to her chin and gently moved her face towards him. From the reflection of the stars on her face, he could tell that she looked sad.

"I'm sorry. Did I say something that hurt or bothered you?" he asked. She paused and looked at him briefly.

"No." She answered and then asked, "Have I said anything to hurt you since I've been here?"

"Of course not, Grace! I can't ever remember having this much fun in my entire life. There is no one I want to be with more than you." He reached out to hug her. But she paused for a moment.

She looked into his eyes ever so much deeper than before to see if he was lying to her. After a few moments, she smiled and they hugged.

"I would never want to hurt you on purpose, Brent."

"I know that. I can feel it too. But thank you," he said

with a warm heart and continued.

"It's not that you want to hurt me. But in the end, we are all human beings with weaknesses, with a past that is less than what we had hoped it would be. The question is, does your heart want to hurt me? Is it in revenge-seeking mode? We all make mistakes and sometimes say things that we might regret due to anger or frustration we might feel at that one particular time."

"But it's always about the bigger picture. Do you really want to be with a certain person? Why? It's because of how they make you feel when you are with them. Like being special, unique, that you matter in their life... and are needed and wanted. Then somewhere down the road, because you are together, you begin to realize that when you are not with them, you feel a touch of emptiness on the inside because you long for their companionship."

"Most people strive for perfection in a mate, yet don't see or wish to see where they fall short of it in their own lives. And sadly enough most don't really care to improve themselves either. So, if that is what someone is looking for in a mate, then they will look for the rest of their lives and never find that perfection because it's just not there. However, if you are looking for someone to grow old with, to seek out more of the things you are wanting to do, to have, to be, to conqueror, then that is a recipe for success. Forgiveness, while being humble from both sides, is usually what works." Brent concludes;

"In my world, love is giving to another person, without expecting in return. Hoping that it will be returned, yes. But not expecting it. You want to give them the best you can provide for them. You give not to receive back, but give because that person means so much to you that you really want to do and says things that make them happy. That enhances their life, that helps them, to bring joy and fulfillment into their being. So I believe love is giving of yourself to someone. Giving of your thoughtful and uplifting words. Doing for them in actions because that is what you want to do."

Grace turned to him in shock.

"OK. That is some heavy stuff to be saying on a second date, you know."

"Sorry, it just came out."

Grace chuckled.

"Don't be sorry. I agree with you."

They snuggled the best they could in the car and looked up for a long while. There was that peace again that she gave him that brought so much comfort and joy into his life. *Two peas in a pod*, he thought. They talked off and on throughout the night. Hours later, they sped off so he could drop her off at the hotel for the night. Or should we say in the morning. It was 2:00 am.

Chapter 7

Sunday morning was a tough one for Brent. He got into his convertible and put a small package onto the floor in the back. He pulled out of his driveway and went to pick up Grace from the hotel. She was scheduled to leave on an afternoon flight. There wasn't much time left to spend with her. He knew this could possibly happen before she came out to see him - she had taken his heart. And she wasn't going to give it back. But now, she was going back home to her life.

How could anyone take my heart so quickly? Maybe she's supposed to have control of it at this stage of my life. I have to admit that I've respected her since the first day I saw her.

He definitely had strong feelings for her, and they were growing too! He felt she did for him too. But more than likely, she won't say anything because she still wanted to get to know him better. He pulled up to the hotel by the front door and got out. He went to the phone in the lobby to call and tell her that he was there. As the phone started to ring, she appeared in the lobby.

"Well, good morning. Did you sleep well last night?" he asked, hanging up the phone.

"Good morning to you too. Yes, I did. Come up with me if you would. I'm not quite ready yet."

They turned and headed toward the elevator. He pressed the fifth floor button and the elevator started to go up.

"So, Grace, are you ready for breakfast?"

Grace paused, "Ah, sorry, but I already kind of ate. I got hungry and helped myself to the continental breakfast they had downstairs."

Now Brent paused because he was caught off guard with her answer. He was looking forward to having breakfast with her. He started to wonder, but continued so she didn't pick on his disappointment.

"So, how was the food? Anything worth eating?" To his surprise, she didn't answer him.

They got off the elevator and approached her door. She inserted her swipe card and entered. She then turned to him and stated, "Well, you can see for yourself! I went down and got this just before you arrived."

On the only table across the room was a good size mixture of food from downstairs. There were eggs, a couple of donuts, sausage, pancakes, and fruit. "I didn't know what you liked, so I got a little of everything. Is this ok?"

Brent looked at the setting and smiled. "This will be just fine. Thank you."

Grace continued, "I thought I would bring it upstairs so we could have breakfast together, alone! Oh, what I meant by having breakfast already was I nibbled a little on the fruit. It was good too!"

That comment warmed his heart. They sat down and started to eat. *I see life around her is very exciting at times!*

"I see why you 'nibbled' a little on the fruit. It looks great, Grace."

"I had something else in mind for breakfast. However, I

have to say, I like this a whole lot better!"

As they were eating, Grace spoke up and said, "I sensed that you were a little disappointed about my eating by your hesitation a few moments ago in the elevator…"

Brent looked up into her eyes and nodded.

"Looks like I can't hide too many things from you…"

She just smiled. "I can read you like a book, so to speak…" she continued.

After they were done eating, Brent looked around and noticed she wasn't finished packing yet.

She then got up and went to the bathroom. His thoughts drifted into sadness thinking how much he was going to miss her.

She poked her head out of the bathroom to see what he was doing. She saw him looking rather pensive. "Ok, Mr. Gentleman, a penny for your thoughts. I know that look on your face. What are you thinking about now? …. Please?" She smiled with that charm only she could give off.

"I was just thinking about how much I'm going to miss you. That's all. You know, the more I find out about you, the more I like you just the way you are."

"Hmmm, I can check that one off too!" she said from the bathroom.

Brent shook his head thinking. She *makes life rather interesting to experience, I have to admit.*

"Ok, where's that list that contains all these things you have to find out about me? I'd like to see it. How long is it, three or four pages? Is it in a spreadsheet or something??"

She poked her head out of the bathroom, smiled and pointed to her head with her index finger. Her eyebrows moved up as she smiled, turned, and continued putting her makeup on. They laughed together again.

"So, Ms. Jokes, for any occasion, did YOU get enough sleep last night?"

She poked her head out of the bathroom and turned to him saying, "Well, it's interesting you should ask. I got to bed really late last night. Or should I say this morning. The reason is that I was watching a movie. And boy was it a sexy one. It was about these two people that went out on the town and had a really great time. They made fools of themselves at a Chinese restaurant. As they were driving around, they almost had an accident because they were laughing so hard that the driver couldn't see the road."

"Oh, really? Sounds like an interesting movie. What happened next?" he asked her.

"Well, he managed to get off the road before they had an accident. And they wound up staying where they parked for hours, talking and having a great time looking at the stars through the open roof in his foreign sports car. I think it starts with a B... something. Oh yeah, BMW. What I thought was disappointing in the movie was the part where she offered to help him drive by sitting in his lap and steering the car. But he didn't take her up on her offer."

His eyes opened wide in astonishment, and he smiled. *She's a blast. Wow!*

"Then what? Did he make the move on her?" Brent asked.

"Nope." She said with disappointment.

"What kind of guy doesn't get the hint on something like that?" Brent sheepishly asked.

She poked her head out of the bathroom. "Well, my guess is he's a gentleman," she said with a wink and returned to the bathroom.

"Oh, I see. What was I thinking? So what happened next?" Brent asked.

"Well, even though he didn't take advantage of the situation like she wanted him to, she really grew to respect him for his self-restraint." She walked out of the bathroom still talking. "So what happened is she was an old-fashioned gal and really grew to respect and trust him more than what she thought she could. She had a great romantic evening with him without any sex involved. And that impressed her greatly. She had a checklist for him. That one earned a big check mark in the good column," she said as her charm came out and she smiled again.

"Wow. That movie sounds familiar. How did it end?" Brent asked.

"Well, I didn't watch it all. It was getting late and I didn't want to stay up too late. I wanted to be with you so I knew I needed the sleep. I turned it off around 2:00 am."

Is she trying to tell me something or what?

They proceeded to leave her room and the hotel for the final time. It was bittersweet. He thoroughly enjoyed her conversational skills. She never failed to amaze him with her words or deeds.

He put her luggage in the trunk. Again, he opened the car door for her. Then he got in.

She grabbed his hand, looked into his eyes and said, "I'm going to miss having the door opened for me all the time. It really makes me feel special. You know, I could get used to this being done for me all the time. Thank you for the experience. I'll remember it for a long time!"

His eyes moisten as he said; "It's my pleasure to do that for a lady! You know, that's the only rule I have in this car." She grinned and kept holding his hand and squeezing it so gently while he squeezed hers. They drove off and headed to his place.

Brent started to think about Grace making her flight on time. "We need to leave by 3:00 to make your flight. We'll call the airline to make sure it's leaving when it's supposed once we get to my house."

She nodded and was silent for a while. Her eyes got moist. He looked after every detail for her stay. It moved her heart in such a way that it made her sad to know it was coming to an end today. When they arrived at his place, they found themselves on the back porch sitting together, not saying much.

He chirped up and reached into his pocket. He pulled out

a penny and said, "Penny for your thoughts, if you don't mind ... please. Does that sound familiar?"

She didn't say anything to him for a while. So he patiently waited for her to respond. They cuddled together on the glider like two peas in a pod.

"I'm just reflecting on what has happened and what the future will hold. You never know what will happen, do you?"

"Yeah. I was thinking the same thing, Grace. You know, you haven't talked much about your baby who died when he was an infant. Anything you want to share?"

She was shocked. "How did you know I was thinking about that?"

"Well, I don't want to scare you, but I picked up on your emotions. I could feel your pain and sorrow that was associated with it just now. You have a heavy heart concerning it. That didn't bother you did it? I mean me picking up on and reading your emotions..."

"Ah, no. I was just surprised by it. Can you do that a lot with people?"

He paused. "Well, most of the time, I can. It all depends. Sometimes, I pick up on too many things from people. It can get a little unsettling. I have to try to turn it off. Hey, let's take a walk down the white wooden path before we leave."

"Sure!"

They both start walking down the path. There are huge rocks on both sides of the path. But as they continue to walk, a beach appears as the lake water laps up onto the sandy colored beach.

"Wow. This is so beautiful."

They just stand there for a few moments.

"Say, if you don't mind me asking, Brent, are you planning on moving back to my area in the future?"

Brent didn't answer right away. So she waited patiently for a response. "Well, I never thought about it until a couple of weeks ago. But, I have been thinking about it, yes. It all depends on if I have a reason to move. So right now, I'm

considering it. Why do you ask, Grace?"
She looked into his eyes before she answered. And with that look, she answered his question. Another smile appeared on his face.
She looked into his eyes again and hugged him. The tears from his eyes started to flow a little then. "I'd wipe them for you if you want, but I don't have any Kleenex on me at the moment. Hey, forget the Kleenex. Here, I'll use this..." She gently wiped the tears with her soft hand. He grabbed her hand and gently kissed it. Her eyes became softer.
"You did wash your hands recently, right?" he asked jokingly.
"Yep, sur nuf did, mister. I washed dur hands this past Friday fore I boarded dur plane!" They looked at each other for a moment and busted out laughing. This whole weekend was so magical for both of them.
He grabbed her hand and looked at his watch. She saw the time too. The great times they were having together were coming to an end. They walked back to the glider. He grabbed the cordless phone from the table next to it and called the airline. Her flight was scheduled to leave on time with no delays. He turned and looked at her. It was about time to leave for the airport. Sadness settled over them. They didn't have to look into each other's eyes to know what the other was feeling.

Chapter 8

They made their way to his car for the final time. He held the driver's side door open for her this time. She stood there, by the front bumper, looking at him. She never drove this kind of sports car before. She froze. She was reluctant to drive it. After a few minutes Brent spoke up.
"Grace, some things in life just need to be experienced. And this is one of them. Most people will never sit in one of

these cars, let alone drive one. Here's your chance to drive one. Don't worry about wrecking it. I'll just go and get another one."

He just stood there waiting for her to get in. She still didn't move. You could tell it was going to be an experience for her to drive it.

After a few more minutes he said, "It's an automatic." There was silence. "Live life without regrets, Grace. You may never get another chance to drive one. Life is about relationships and the experiences you have within those relationships. It has already been a memorable weekend. Top off this fantastic memory we both shared. Please?? It's a convertible..."

He paused then said softly, "You'll look even more beautiful with those gorgeous blue eyes of yours that perfectly match the color of the car!"

With that, she finally looked into his eyes. Then she smiled, slowly moved towards the door and very slowly got in. She was scared, excited, and thrilled beyond measure. He helped her adjust the seat to where she was comfortable. Then he closed the door for her and got in the other side. She adjusted the mirrors and started the car. It roared to life.

"Oh my, this is so nice. I can't get over how soft these leather seats are. I've got goose bumps all over."

He touched her shoulder as if to calm her down. She looked over as if to ask if he was sure about this? He blinked both eyes and smiled in approval. She adjusted the seat a little more and checked the mirrors again. She put it into reverse and backed out of the driveway. Then she stopped, put it into drive and pushed the accelerator. The car darted down the street.

"Oh my gosh, this is thrilling to feel and...." she didn't finish. She didn't need to. He understood completely what she felt. They were off to the airport.

After a third of the way to the airport, she spoke up. "I don't know about you, but I think a tremor is starting up again. Can you call the weather service to see if there are any earthquakes have been detected in this immediate area?" He shook his head and laughed some.

"Hey, we can do better than that. Let's check out the weather band channel. It's SO exciting to hear them talk," he said sarcastically.

But that was her hint that she was getting hungry. What a sense of humor he thought. *Who is this woman who captured my heart?*

She continued. "So you have the weather band radio in this car. Where's the cable TV? Could I be driving too fast to get a good reception? You know, I think a hot tub right here would be just great. That way I could drive, soak, and relax all at the same time. How much was that option?"

He laughed and cried at the same time. He laughed because the jokes were funny and the timing was so great, but he cried inside because he wouldn't hear them again for a very long time, if ever.

"There is an earthquake reporting station over there on the left side of the road. Is that a good enough place for you, Grace?"

He pointed to a fast-food restaurant. She smiled and turned on the blinker.

He continued, "You may want to let me out before you go through the drive-through. They almost never get the order right when I'm in the car."

She laughed and shared her stories about how many times her food orders got messed up. As she placed their order at the drive-through, he took a little envelope out of his jacket pocket, when she wasn't looking, and placed it into her purse, which was between them.

They left the drive-through and approached the on-ramp to the expressway. "Are you comfortable driving it yet?" he asked.

"Oh, yes. I could get used to this very easily. Am I doing ok?"

"You're doing just great. I'm completely comfortable with your driving. As to you driving this car a lot more often, well, be careful what you wish for, Grace, you might get it. You never know what might happen." He paused to see what her reaction would be.

"Now, when you get on the on-ramp over here, floor it and enjoy."

"Ah ... ok," She did. The car jumped forward instantly pushing both of them back in their seats. Before they were halfway up the ramp, they were at the speed limit and beyond.

"Oh, my gosh, what a thrill ... I'm feeling a little strange. I never felt like this before. What is that feeling?" she asked.

"That's adrenaline. This car will give you a rush like that. This is what race-car drivers feel sometimes when they are in their funny cars, dragsters, or open-wheel racing cars. It's great, isn't it?"

She nodded. *What a thrill*, she thought. *This whole weekend was a dream.* Now she had to go back to life as normal. *It'll seem so dull.*

As they drove on the expressway, he opened her hamburger and gave it to her.

"Thank you" she said pleasantly as she took a bite.

"You're welcome. But try keeping the ketchup and onion off the seats," he jokingly stated.

When she heard that, she about lost it and almost spit the food in her mouth all over the dash.

"Careful there, dear. I don't want the onions going down the heater vents. It would make for an interesting smell in the wintertime. On the other hand, it might make me hungry for one of those small hamburgers! On second thought, don't worry about it."

They both were having a great time. He fed her some French fries and then the second hamburger while she was driving.

"I can't believe we're eating in your car."

"Well, why not, Grace? It's only a car. Are you having a good time with all this?" She stopped eating for a moment, turned and just looked in his eyes. Yes. Without a doubt, she was.

"Great, then that's more important than this car. It's the experience we are having together that really counts, isn't it?" She stopped munching for a few moments and nodded. He could see the emotion in her eyes.

They finished eating their lunch. "I know what can top this off! And it's one of the major food groups too! Let's see, I think I'd like..." she stated quite smoothly.

As she was talking, he smiled and reached around on the floor of the back seat. He pulled out a small box. He showed it to her. It was a small box of chocolates - her favorite. He opened it for her. Tears appeared in her eyes.

"You... you... got those for...." She didn't need to finish her statement. He understood.

The rest of the trip to the airport was quiet. His heart hurt and ached so bad that he could feel his heart beat. She reached out and grabbed his hand and squeezed it. She had tears in her eyes.

They made it to the airport, and she parked the car in the parking garage. "Ok, since I'm driving, I think I should open your door for you. That's the rule in our car, I mean, your car!"

She flashed that look and charm at him. *I'll give her an A+ for delivery and original thinking. Ah, why not.*

"Ok, go ahead. Make it look good, but don't get any fingerprints on the paint, please." She got out and opened the door for him.

He got out and jokingly said, "You know, I could get used to this sort of thing!"

She then started putting her palm prints all over the painted area of the car door then on top of the hood. He looked at the car, then at her and said, "I won't wash that part of the car until I see you again."

"Oh, really" she said. "Is there someone else that's going to be opening the door for you like that?"

"Well there is this lady I know…" Brent couldn't hold it in and started to laugh.

"No."

"Good. I mean, I'm sorry that no one thought enough about you to do that for you."

He said, "Are you getting your luggage out of the trunk too? I mean really, seeing how you started this scenario, you should do that too, right?"

She chuckled, but Brent opened the trunk and grabbed her luggage before she could get it. They started to walk together, holding hands. She pushed the button to set the alarm.

"Well, you can have these back, dear." She handed him the keys. He looked at them and waited a few moments. He raised his eyes to hers. It hurt to get them back from her. He slowly opened his left hand to take them back. She slowly put them into his hand and closed it for him. Then she held onto it for a while. They didn't say a word until they got into the airport. They just enjoyed each other's presence.

They approached the ticket agent, and she checked-in.

"Hey, Grace, let's go to one of the shops here."

She said, "Sure! I like window shopping!!"

They entered a gift shop. She found a little bear that had the airport's name and the city on it. It was rather cute. It was dressed in denim. Grace liked it, so he bought it for her.

"Now you have something to remember this visit." Brent said.

She held it close to her chest, right over her heart. Then they both sat down for a while on a two-seated couch in the airport. They held hands. Tears flowed from both their eyes. They hardly said a word. Finally, it was time for her to go through security and to the terminal.

"When are you coming out to see me, Brent?"

Chapter 9

"I'm not sure. When do you want me to come and visit?"
"How about right this moment? Some of my friends would love to meet you."
He looked down. She knew he couldn't come with her. They both stood up and walked over to the walkway. They hugged for the final time at the security checkpoint. This embrace might be the last one they would share for a long time or maybe forever. Right before they let go, he whispered something very sweet in her ear.
"I'll see you tonight."
She looked into his eyes one last time. Tears flowed from her eyes like a river now. She gave him another squeeze. She knew what he meant. He would see her in his dreams. With that, she started to turn and go to the terminal. She walked away for a few moments, but stopped, turned around and ran back, jumping into his arms. And they kissed. It was the first time they had ever kissed. Then she turned and walked away. She never looked back as he intensely watched her until she disappeared from sight.
She got on the plane and found her seat next to the window. Her mind was reeling from one of the most memorable weekends in her entire life. She turned and looked out the window into what was seemingly a daze.
Was this all a dream? If it was, I don't want to wake up. Who is this old friend whom I have known for many years? It has been so long since I've seen him. I thought he was a great person from what I knew of him, but I didn't know what type of a person he really was. Now what do I do? I've just been with a man who is a women's dream. But I wonder if that's what he's really like? I have to admit, he seemed genuine. I didn't sense he was being phony or putting on a front.
She paused as the plane pulled away from the terminal. She could see the terminal as the plane turned and taxied

towards the runway. Then it began to accelerate as it started to reach the proper air speed. She started to feel the unevenness of the runway as her body bounced some. The speed continued to increase. Within a matter of seconds, the ride became smoother as the plane lifted off and became airborne. As it started to circle to go home, it banked, and she got one last glance at the airport. Tears streamed down her cheeks. She put her hand up to the window and said,
"Good-bye. Thank you!"

As the plane continued to climb to the proper cruising altitude, the airport was soon out of sight. She continued to look out the window. She remembered the relationships she had had in the past, along with a marriage that only lasted for a few years. She really hadn't had a serious relationship for a long time. She seemingly didn't have very good luck with men.

Could he be different than other men? Usually men want one thing (sex) and are controlling. But I didn't see or feel anything like that from him. Oh my, my mind is just going in circles now. Maybe I shouldn't have come here. But now I want to get to know him better. But how can I? We live so far apart. How can two people have a relationship and get to know each other over such a long distance? I don't want to get hurt again. As much as I wanted to, I couldn't open my heart to him. Well, this was the first time we saw each other after so many years with no contact. But, on the other hand, I'm glad we found each other again in that internet chat room. It was a fantastic weekend. Well, one thing is for certain - our friendship seemed to pick up right where we left off ten years ago. And my heart fluttered so many times when we were together. I guess I felt like a teenager again ... if there is such a feeling like that.

Her heart was heavy, and her mind was confused by the experience she had this weekend. Her tears continued to flow, and she tried to wipe them from her cheeks and eyes as she looked out the window. But she couldn't stop crying. She turned away from the window and reached into her purse, trying to find a tissue. She couldn't find one.

Great, I'm making a fool of myself in public, and I can't find a tissue.

She finally found one and wiped her eyes. She sat quietly in her seat, holding the little bear he bought her at the airport. She looked at it as she held it on her lap. She slowly brought it up to her chest lightly embracing it. The wonderful memories from this weekend brought tears again.

She put the bear back on her lap and looked for a breath mint. Then she found the envelope he had placed in her purse. She didn't know it was from him, but she didn't remember putting it in her purse either. She pulled it out. It had two words on the envelope,

'Thank You'.

She put her right hand over her mouth while holding it in her left hand. She wasn't sure what to do. *Where did this come from?* She was flabbergasted and caught completely off guard. She just looked at it for a few moments. Then she turned the envelope over and slowly opened it. It had a card inside. On the front, it said,

To the Lady I call 'Amazing Grace'!

She opened it. It looked like a standard greeting card, but it wasn't something you would buy at the store. It read:

"To a beautiful lady! I wanted to make a card for you. I made it on my computer last night after I dropped you off. I want to thank you for coming to see me this weekend. I don't know if you had mixed feeling about coming at first, but I think you were glad you came for many reasons. Thank you for touching my life like you have done. It's been a long time since I felt so ... alive and wanted by someone. I would like to come and see you in the very near future, if that is ok with you. I believe you would like that. Please let me know, at your convenience, so I can be sure."

As she read the card, her mouth dropped open in total amazement. Her mind was spinning big time now. She started to realize that there was more to Brent than what she knew. She looked at the bear and kissed it. The tears started to flow again. Just then, she heard the voice of the man sitting next to her.

She wiped the tears from her eyes the best she could and said to him, "Excuse me? I didn't hear what you said."

"Have you had that bear for very long?" he said softly.

Being slightly puzzled by the question, she looked at him and started to make a comment. However, she suddenly stopped before she had spoken another word. She was astonished and taken back. Then her mouth dropped open. She looked away and turned back again.

"I'm sorry, but you are looking at me like I'm a ghost or something," he said in a questioning voice.

She swallowed hard and tried to figure out what to say. "Well, forgive me, but you look like someone I know. As a matter of fact, you could be his twin brother. I was just visiting this wonderful man whom I haven't seen for many years. I've had the time of my life with him. Right now, I'm actually missing him. So, I'm sorry if I offended you."

"Oh, that's ok. My name is Andy."

"I'm pleased to meet you. I'm Grace." She continued, "Why did you ask me if I'd had the bear for very long?"

"Well, my company sells stuffed animals like that." Andy stated, as a matter of fact.

"Oh, no kidding? What a coincidence this is," she added with a little charm.

He continued, "Did you know what that bear stands for? Most of these types of bears have a hidden meaning with them. Some stand for friendship, some for missing you, others for love and romance, or budding romance. People usually don't know these things."

"Oh, really? I never knew that." That started her thinking. "Ok. Can you tell me what this bear stands for?"

"Sure. This is a special-edition bear for a certain city or area. This is usually sold only in airports. This is a hug me bear."

"Oh, wow. That's great. We picked this one out together. Thank you!"

"You're welcome. And thanks for buying one. It'll help pay my salary," he said with a little smile. She smiled back. Then her mind drifted back to their last hug.

Gosh, it's hard to imagine how we picked this specific type of bear. What memories I have to remember. Well, I just want to make sure he is this wonderful man whom I've seen so far. I can't let him have control over my heart. On the other hand, it hurts. When I've done this in the past, it's never turned out the way I thought it would.

Before she knew it, the plane was starting to land at the airport near her home. *Back to reality... but it doesn't feel the same - like it used it...*

She arrived safely. She got her luggage and headed to her car and home. On the way home, she called Brent's home number from her cell phone to let him know she was home safely and would be very happy to have him come out and visit. He didn't answer, so she left a message on his answering machine.

"Hi, Brent, it's me. I just wanted to let you know that I arrived safely at the airport. I had a wonderful weekend with you. Call me when you get this message."

Grace didn't want to tell him about her feelings. She was still unsure about the feelings and emotions she was experiencing at this point in their relationship.

Brent's ride home was hard. He waited until the plane took off before heading back to his car. After leaving the parking garage, he made his way to the highway and home. He was sorrowful that she is not with him, but thankful they had these days together. His thoughts were about her. He felt numb. He wasn't sure what or how to feel. He turned on the radio for some comfort. They were playing a song, "Can you hold me for all time? Can I, can I have this kiss, FOREVER?" After hearing that, he turned the radio off and drove to the rest area they were at the night before. He sat there remembering her and feeling empty - like he was alone again.

Grace finally got home and put her luggage and purse down on the floor in the kitchen. As soon as she unpacked and settled down in the living room, the phone rang.

I bet it's Brent!

She walked to the phone on the end table and looked at the caller ID - not him. It was Beth. Grace was a little disappointed, but she was glad it was Beth and answered it.

"Hellooooo!"

"Hey, Grace. I see you made it back. How were the flights there and back? How did it go? What did you do? Where did you eat?" she said with nervous excitement.

"Hi, Beth! Yes, I'm back. Everything went great ... maybe too great! My head is swimming in circles. I've got so many things going through my mind, I don't know what to think. You know I'm just starting to think, well, I might look into transferring to the office in his area if this continues... By the way, how did you know I was home?"

"I'm so glad things went well. It sure sounds like you had a fantastic time. You are going to have to fill me in on all the...." Beth paused and then continued. "Hold on, lady. Did you say what I think you said? You are thinking about moving? What did he do, ask you to... Wait, I'll be over there in a few minutes. I'm walking out the door right now. I'll bring something to eat with me."

Before Grace could say anything, she heard a dial tone. She really wanted to be alone to try to sort things out, but she realized that wasn't going to happen.

Beth arrived about twenty minutes later with food, a bunch of questions and a hug.

"So, welcome back. I have so many questions to ask you. Obviously, you had an interesting time to say the least. I gathered that by our earlier phone conversation." Grace just grinned.

They sat down at the kitchen table and started eating. Beth continued.

"Ok. I should allow you to talk first, but I can't wait on this one. Well, I have a couple of questions to start off with at least. My first question, is he a hunk?"

Grace smiled at her. "Well, he is really hot. He's a man who is in touch with his feelings. But he has this other side that's masculine too. He's really sexy too!"

"Ok, number two, does he have a lot of money?" Grace looked at her a little puzzled and hurt by the question. "Hey, I was just asking. If this becomes really serious, you won't have to work, right?"

"I don't want him to support me. I'm not after his possessions. I'm interested in him. However, if you must know, he owns his home and his car, well cars. And the one I drove was something else. I had a blast with it. I thought if I pressed the wrong button I might be ejected from the car," she said with a big smile.

She signed and continued.

"I connected to him so quickly. He is just..." Grace couldn't finish that sentence. She continued to talk Beth's ear off most of the evening about what had happened and the fun she had being with him.

Chapter 10

That evening, as Stan was walking to the locker room, another officer walked by and stopped.

Hey, Stan, the Sergeant wants to talk to you."

"Oh, really? Do you know why?"

"No. He didn't say. But he wants to see you right now. That's all I know."

"Thanks."

Stan turned and walked down another hallway. He stopped at the door that said 'Sergeant Lester Grey'. He knocked on the glass.

"Come in."

"Hey, Sergeant, you wanted to see me?"

"Yes, I do, Stan. Close the door and take a seat."

He closed the door and sat down.

"I've been going over your record, Stan. You have a long career of excellence since you've been here. And it's appreciated. However, I've gotten some reports about you in the last six weeks or so. They are a little cause of concern for me. How are things going?"

"I'm not sure I understand the question, sir. I'm doing ok, Sergeant."

"Are you sure?"

"What's this all about, sir?"

"I've been getting some reports about some changes in your attitude. It's becoming very negative, and it seems like it's becoming hostile."

"Hostile sir? Who's been saying that, sir?"

"It's coming from some of your fellow officers. I noticed it the other day myself. So, do you want to tell me what's going on? Are you not happy here? Are you having troubles at home?"

"Well, I am having a bit of a problem with the wife at home. But I'm trying not to bring it to work with me."

"Mind telling me what's going on, Stan?"

"Well, sir, I'd rather keep it to myself, if you don't mind."

"We are paid to do a tough, thankless job. We see things that others don't. And they can affect anyone, including me. So, if this situation you have at home is spilling over into your professional career, then we have a problem and it needs to be addressed."

"I've gotten a handle on it, sir."

"Do you know? I don't think you are handling it well at all."

"I beg to differ with you, sir!"

"Well, you can think what you want. But what I think

goes when it comes to who I send out onto the streets. And right now, I'm this close to giving you temporary desk duties until this situation works itself out."

The Sergeant got out of his chair and sat on the corner of his desk, closer to Stan.

"Stan, you are a great cop. Your record speaks for itself. You should be proud of it. But if your personal life is interfering with your duties, then I'm going to take you off the streets. I'm going to order you to get some professional help. I'm concerned Stan, ok? I'm concerned and I want to help."

"Thanks for your concern, Sergeant, but I don't think I need the counseling right now."

"I think you do. I don't want, shall I say, a "Dirty Harry" on the streets in my district." He paused and then continued.

"Stan, right now I'm talking to you man to man. Are you sure you don't want to tell me what's going on? You don't have to tell me. That's your right. But if you don't, then you're off the streets until this is worked out. It's your choice."

Stan looked at the Sergeant and looked down at the floor.

"My wife and I are having some marital issues. I think she's having an affair. More than likely, I think we might be getting a divorce."

The Sergeant nodded his head slightly.

"Being a cop's wife is tough. I know, because I'm married too. So, level with me Stan, are you ok to be out there on the streets?"

"I think so; but, how about this for a solution. If I think I'm starting to lose it, I'll come to you, and then we'll talk about me taking a desk job. How is that, Sergeant?"

"Are you on the level with me?"

"Yes, sir."

He sat back down in his chair.

"Ok, Stan. I'll agree to that. I'm still not sure if I'm

doing you a favor by doing this, but I'll give you the benefit of the doubt. But if I see anything that I don't like, it's desk duty for you. Are we clear?"

"Yes, sir." Stan said while nodding his head.

"Ok, get out of here and guard the taxpayers like we are supposed to do."

Stan got up and opened the door. He turned his head slightly towards the Sergeant.

"Thanks."

The Sergeant nodded his head in acknowledgment and closed the file on his desk. Stan left the room.

He walked to the locker room and sat down on the bench in front of his locker. He just sat there starring at the lockers. The locker room door opened, and George walked in. He went to his locker, which was almost right next to Stan's. He noticed that Stan was just sitting there in a trance. He stopped and walked over to him.

"Hey, Stan. Are you OK?"

Stan didn't say a word. George sat down next to him and waited. He folded his hands, put his forearms on his thighs and looked at the floor.

"Well, the lovely wife is cheating on me now. I drove home early yesterday and found one of those blue sports cars parked in front of my house. I pulled down the street and waited to see if the owner was in my house. Sure enough, a man came out of my house, got into that car and sped off. I waited about fifteen minutes and then pulled into my driveway. I asked my wife how her day was going. She said fine. But she seemed ... distant." After saying that, he just sat there starring at his locker, shaking his head back and forth.

George paused and then asked, "Did you check out the license plate on the car?"

"Yes, I did. It was some guy from a neighboring town. He was clean. He's a professional man. I think he might be a doctor."

"Is there anything I can do for you, Stan?"

"No. I know she's not happy being with me. But I didn't think this would happen ... now."

Stan started remembering all the arrests he had made and started to talk. "We so often see the depravity of man, the dregs, the lowlifes, and the lowest possible gutter that man can find himself sitting in. The very people we are sworn to protect, sometimes with our own lives, often curse us when we pull them over for a simple traffic violation."

Stan continued. "Sometimes I wonder when we are babysitting and when we are actually protecting and serving. At times, I wonder if the worse of the traffic offenders aren't the politicians. I often wonder if some of them think they are above the law. Yet, these same people don't hesitate to call us when they are in trouble and need assistance. Yes, that's the job, but it's difficult to see the same type of paradox in any other job in the world. So much for job satisfaction, huh, George? How much longer do I want to continue to do this? What else can I do in this age of computers and high-tech equipment? You know, I went into the academy right after getting my bachelor's degree."

Stan got up and started to pace back and forth continuing to reflect on the past.

"I wanted to make a difference like my dad, and my grandfather did, George. I remember when my grandfather would talk about his experiences when he was the Chief of Police. I sat there glued to my seat for hours as he talked about some of the criminals and villains he apprehended and the impact he made by helping to make a difference in his community. Maybe that's when my life's work was set in stone. He joined the police force right before World War II. He talked about how difficult it was during the Great Depression and how lucky he was to get a job as a cop right after the war. Back in those days, people showed their respect to police officers. Kids weren't afraid of them either because their parents taught them to be respectful. They were revered as a friend. So when you were in trouble, you could go to one to help you."

Stan leaned with his back against the lockers looking at George, who sat there not saying a word, but listened intently to some of Stan's family history.

"They weren't called pigs or anything remotely like that back then. But according to my grandfather, that started to change in the late fifty or early sixtie It seems like it's getting worse now. Society back then didn't have all the problems with drugs either, well until the sixties maybe. The most trouble they had was at the local bars. You would almost always have someone who drank too much and got rowdy." Stan paused and continued, "They would take him to jail and let him sleep it off. If he didn't give them a problem and if the bar or anyone else that might be involved didn't press charges, they wouldn't book him. Of course, they always chuckled at the teenagers that got caught doing some harmless pranks. He admitted he had trouble holding back a smile or a big grin when he caught them in the act. After he got his thirty years in, he retired because he saw how society was changing and how it viewed law enforcement so negatively. He lived to a ripe old age of eighty four, George."

Stan started to smile a bit and said, "I was glad he lived long enough to see me graduate from the Academy. It was hard for me to fight back the tears when he showed up at the swearing-in ceremony at City Hall when I was promoted from a cadet to a police officer. He came in full uniform too! He was given so much respect at that ceremony, it was hard fighting back the tears. I wasn't sure if I was more proud of what I had done or for him coming and the respect he was shown."

Stan started to walk around a little bit. "The advancements with fingerprints, photography, and DNA technology has made tracking and catching criminals so much easier. We now have a better chance of catching the right person. But I remember my grandfather mentioning to me that he didn't want me to pursue this line of work. When I asked him why he joined, he began to remember why he chose to pursue what he thought was his lifelong work. But, he never really gave me a direct answer to my question."

Stan sat down again, looked at the locker and smiled a bit.

"I remember my first patrolman's job in the small town of Carmeltown, George. Everyone knew everyone and everybody's business. I have to laugh a little bit about that. Such idealism I had when I first joined the force. What happened to me after these twenty two years of serving the public, buddy? My life seems like a shambles. I can't seem to keep my wife happy. I have these nightmares of what I have experienced. What am I doing? Do I need to find another career so I can have a life? How do you do it, George? I can't go home and share what happened at work with my wife. Do you? Some of the things are downright awful to say the very least. I can't really share anything I do with her like I could in a normal marriage."

Stan paused again for a few moments and then continued.

"I'm sorry, George. I don't expect an answer from you. I'm just struggling with trying to make sense of all that's happening at the moment. It hurts really bad, and I don't know what to do."

There was silence for a few minutes. George started to speak up and say something, but changed his mind and just stood there.

"Well, it's time to get out there a make the county some money from people trying to take liberties by exceeding the speed limit," Stan said. George paused and then nodded his head and went to his locker.

Chapter 11

The next evening, Brent made himself supper and sat in front of the TV watching a movie. He remembered his time with Grace. His heart ached inside. He longed to continue making memories with her. He had some hope because she had called him stating she wanted him to come out and see her. But he missed her so much that he didn't eat much of his supper. As he was thinking, he heard a noise from outside. It was a car pulling into the driveway. *Who is that in my driveway?*

Brent got up from his chair and headed for the front door, which was open. A lady approached his front door. It was his daughter Carol.

"Hi, Carol!"

"Hi, Dad. How are you doing? How did the weekend go?"

"Come on in and have a seat. Are you hungry? Did you have supper yet?"

"I'm fine, Dad. I ate before I came over."

"Ok. Well, have a seat. I was just finishing up my supper."

They both walked over to the TV area and sat down. Carol looked at her Dad and noticed he was acting slightly subdued. Her excitement to see him and anxiousness to hear about his weekend began turning to worry. She noticed he hadn't eaten much of his supper. After observing him for a few moments, she became slightly apprehensive.

Brent reached for the remote and turned off the TV. He mustered up a fake smile, but it quickly vanished.

Her concern grew. "Dad…"

He looked over to Carol and saw her concern. "Carol … it was a fantastic weekend, honey. It's been so long since I felt that good. I actually miss her now. I'm sorry. I'm probably not good company right now."

Carol sat back in the chair and pondered what to say. She decided to just wait and see what he said next.

Brent turned and looked down. His eyes were slightly moist. He didn't say anything.

Carol turned her head and gazed at the dark TV. It was

hard for her to see her Dad like that. She wanted to comfort him, but wasn't sure how to. She started to think about her last relationship and how it felt when she was with him. But she couldn't relate to her dad's feelings because she never felt that way about a man ... yet.

Brent felt her apprehension. "Sorry, Carol. I don't mean to get you upset."

"Oh, that's ok, Dad. I'm just concerned. I guess I don't know what to say. How did you two ... I guess I want to say 'get along'? Do you think you will get together again?"

"Well, Carol, she wants me to come for a visit. So, I'm going to see her in a few weeks, I guess." He paused for a few moments and then continued. "I can't wait to see her again."

Carol started to smile. "So you think there might be something to this, this relationship with her?"

"Well, I don't know. But I'm going to see what develops."

"Do you want to tell me what happened and how this lady turned your heart to mush, so to speak?"

Brent gave her a glance.

She continued. "Come on, Dad. It's written all over your face."

"Is it now? Where is an eraser when you need one...?" Brent said after a fleeting glance at his daughter. She smiled back at him.

"Are you sure you want to know how it went?"

"Yes, sir, I do!"

Brent paused for a few moments. He turned his chair towards her. Brent started to smile brightly. He shared with her the events over the weekend.

"Well, Dad, thanks for sharing that experience with me. It sounds like it was a wonderful time." She paused.

"Hopefully, I'll be able to have that kind of experience for myself someday! Do you think, if it works out, you might move closer to her?"

"I hope you will be able to experience that too." He paused. "I don't know, Carol. I control my own destiny. So we'll see what happens."

They both sat there not saying a word.

"Well, daughter, it's getting late and we both have to go to work in the morning." Brent and Carol both got up and headed toward the door.

"Good night, Dad. Pleasant dreams."

"Same to you, Carol. Watch yourself driving home. Ok?"

"Ok. I'll be by later in the week. Love you."

"Love you too, baby!"

She smiled and nodded her head in acknowledgement as she left. She got in her car and backed down the driveway and onto the street. Brent, standing in the doorway, waved as the car disappeared from site. He closed the front door.

Brent and Grace continued to email back and forth. Sometimes on the weekends, they would talk on the phone. However, she never told him how she felt about their relationship, even though he dropped her some hints about his feelings.

Two more weeks went by when she finally asked him on the phone, "When are you coming out to see me? I'm impatiently waiting for you!! Please tell me you are coming out sooner than what you told me at the airport?"

"I've got a vacation coming up. I'd like to come out then if that's ok with you. It's at the end of this month. How's that?" he asked.

"That will be fine, I guess. I was hoping it would be sooner than that, Brent."

She didn't tell him that most of her thoughts everyday were about him, although it almost slipped out a couple of times. But she didn't want to show how she felt yet. Brent wasn't about to tell her that she was on his mind all the time either. He didn't want to express his feelings because of the fear of rejection.

The end of the month came sooner than they expected. It was finally Tuesday, the day that he was scheduled to leave to go see her. After work, with his bags packed and already in the car, he got into his car and sped off to see Grace. *Maybe she is the next lady in my life - possibly the permanent one?*

The drive seemed to last hours longer than it should. But it was only about four hours. He should know. He had been there many times before. It's where he grew up.

He arrives at the hotel late that night, checked in, and phoned her. When the caller ID showed the call was from the hotel he said he was staying at, she answered quickly. "Hey, honey. How was the trip? Wait, why are you calling from the hotel? I thought you were going to stop here first? I'm impatiently waiting for you..."

After her last words, he stated, "I'm leaving now, darling. See you in a few." He hung up the phone.

He jumped into his car and sped off to meet this fine lady. He pulled into her driveway. She lived in a white, two-story house with aluminum siding and a two-car, detached garage. There were eight windows on the front of the house, two of them were bowed picture windows. The front door was centered on the house with a curved cement walkway running from the driveway to it. Small solar night lights dotted the path all the way to from the driveway to the door. It opened as he approached it. It was 9:30.

They hugged and seemingly picked up right where they left off many weeks ago. Before they knew it, it was 11:30.

"Well, it's time for me to leave, dear, and for both of us to get some sleep. What time do you leave for work?"

"I'm out of the house by 6:30 in the morning. I'm usually home by 6:00. Sorry I can't take time off while you are here. We have a couple of people out sick."

He nodded and told her, "That's ok. I understand. I might have a surprise for you when you get home tomorrow, if that's ok with you."

She jokingly scratched her chin with her fingers saying, "Well, I don't know if I can trust you. Let me think here... Ok, sure. Go ahead and surprise me. Do I get a hint as to what it will be?"

"Of course... NOT! Then it wouldn't be a surprise would it?" Brent said in a matter of fact voice.

She acted like it bothered her, but it really didn't. She handed him the spare key to the front door. He took it and put it on his key ring. Then they hugged and he turned around and headed for his car. He started it up and it roared to life as it always did for him. He pulled out of the driveway and headed to the hotel. She waved as he drove away.

Brent visited some friends the next day while Grace was at work. It had been a long time since he had been there. His friends were all glad to see him.

He arrived at Grace's house around 4:00. He started to prepare supper for her. He knew her favorite foods from their conversations. He was a good cook and enjoyed preparing meals. He had a certain knack for presentation too. He bought the main items from the local grocery store. After looking around the kitchen, he found the rest of what he needed to make the meal. Then he started to put his culinary skills to work so when she came home, she would be able to sit down and eat right away without having to prepare anything.

Around 5:50, Grace pulled into the driveway. She saw his car sitting in front of the garage door. She pushed the garage door opener and pulled in past his car. She got out and walked past his car, smiling, and up to the side door.

Brent heard her car and grinned. The side door opened. He could hear her upbeat voice. It echoed throughout the house.

"Hey, is there a man in my..." she didn't finish the sentence. She could smell the aroma of food in the air. It shocked her a little.

"Something smells good. And it smells better than me

right now. Did you open a can of corned beef hash?"

He grinned but didn't answer. He enjoyed her wit and charm. He missed it so much. He was in the kitchen getting the food ready to put on the table. The closer she got to the dining area, the better the smell was.

"Oh my gosh... what did you do? This looks so great!"

She noticed her fine china was on the table and her best cutlery with wine glass goblets. There were two candles on the table that seemed to have just been lit. She heard some of her favorite music in the background. Finally, she walked into the kitchen, and there he stood.

She continued. "Hi, darling. Do we have the mayor coming by tonight? Don't tell me this is just for you and me?"

He grinned as he hugged her. "Ok. I won't tell you then..."

She looked around. All the dishes, pots and pans were clean and put away.

"Well, I can check that one off my list too." She said with a grin. "It's so romantic in here. You did all of this just for me, or us?"

He nodded. "Yes, dear, for us. I hope you like it."

"I do. Well, after smelling all this, I'm starving. What kind of hamburgers are we having tonight?"

"Your favorite ones! So when you are ready, I can start serving supper," he said very politely.

"I'm ready right now. Let me wash my hands. Where's my Butler tonight?" she asked jokingly.

"Oh, I gave him the night off. I am your Butler tonight."

He knew she didn't have a Butler. After she washed her hands, he walked her to the dining room table. He pulled out the chair for her to sit down. "Thank you."

He acknowledged her comment and nodded.

"I'll be right back with our meal." He brought out her favorite dish, fillet minion. It was cooked to perfection. All the juices were sealed in just the way she liked it. Then he brought out the steamed vegetables and warm biscuits. It was all presented in a great arrangement on the plate. Just looking at it made her mouth water.

"Oh my, you are fantastic, honey."

Her eyes watered at the special attention she got from him again. She couldn't believe he went to this much work on his vacation for her.

She spoke up, "Ah, excuse me. Are you trying to spoil me? You know, I could get used to this very easily. Did I ever mention that before....?" she asked with a smile.

He smiled and sat down to her left. "I think I've heard that before, but I can't remember where. I'm sure it'll come to me sooner or later..."

He paused a minute to see if everything was cooked the way she liked it. It was. They enjoyed a great meal together that evening.

After cleaning up the rest of the dishes together, they sat down and talked while watching some TV.

"Hey, Brent, my program is on. Do you mind if we watch it?"

"Of course not. What's the program?"

She told him as she grabbed the remote and changed the channel.

"What's this? This isn't the program that's supposed to be on. What's up with all this?"

It was a new show that made its debut that night, so they decided to watch it. It became rather corny, and they both thought it was stupid.

"Well isn't this a crock..." she said with utter disgust.

They both somewhat laughed at it. And, before they knew it, they were making fun of it and telling each other this should have been done this way or that way. After a while, they started laughing at it a lot.

Brent spoke up, "Hey, I know. We should move to Hollywood and produce our own show. We'll show them how to do it right. The gall of them putting this on TV without our consent. I can't believe it."

They both laughed and started to make fun of the programs on the other channels for a good hour and a half.

It was getting late now. When it was time for him to leave, he told her "I really don't want to leave, but we were up late last night and you need your rest. Same time tomorrow evening?"

"Of course. What's on the menu for tomorrow night, Mr. Brent?"

"Who said I was cooking?" He started to laugh. "Actually, I don't know right now. Do you have a preference?"

"Nothing comes to mind right now…"

"Well, I think I can figure out something before then," he said with a smile.

"Well, I would have liked breakfast in bed. But if I have to wait, I will. You know, this evening is going to be hard to top. But if you want to, I'll be glad to indulge myself with you. Say, why don't you come down to the office? I'd like for you to see where I work and meet some of my co-workers and friends." Deep in her heart, she wanted to show him off. However, she didn't want to tell him that, at least not yet!

"Thanks for the offer. I might take you up on it one of these days. You're not thinking about showing me off are you?" Brent asked.

"Who me?" she gestured in such a way her body language said that wouldn't be a motive for her invitation.

With that, they hugged and said, "pleasant dreams," almost at the exact same moment. They smiled and stared briefly into each other's eyes. Then he left.

She got ready for bed. When she started to climb into bed, she decided to write him a thank-you note. She walked to the kitchen and placed it in an envelope. She put it on the kitchen table so he could read it when he walked in the next day. Then she went to bed. The words on the outside of the envelope were "To My Gourmet Chef/Companion!"

Chapter 12

Thursday morning rolled around. Brent visited with his closest friends during the day while Grace was at work. They, like the others, asked why he wasn't available for dinner. When he started to talk about Grace, they understood but asked,

"When do we get to meet this lovely lady? Bring her with you! You look really happy. I hope it works out for you. You deserve it!!!"

"Someday I will," was always his reply.

Later that afternoon, he stopped at the grocery store to pick up some things for dinner.

Let's see here. What do I make for supper? Ahhh ... pizza - one of her major food groups! Yes, my homemade pizza. I think she'll like it.

He arrived at her house around 4:15 pm. As he was placing the groceries on the kitchen table, he saw the note across the counter and read it. His eyes got a little moist as the words reached his heart. He sat down and enjoyed the moment while thinking about her thoughtfulness. It read:

'Thank you for the lovely meal tonight. You are an amazing man to say the least, my friend. I hope you will stop by my work tomorrow. I can't wait to see you!'

He smiled while putting down the card and started making the pizza. Sure enough, around 5:50, she walked in the door.

"Hey, I'm home... Wait a minute. Something smells really good. I don't know what's going on here, but it's a good thing."

"Hey, Grace, take a guess what it is. You have three guesses and the first two don't count!" he said from the kitchen.

"Well, I don't know. Let's see... Is it liver and onions?"

"Nope."

"Ok, is it last week's leftovers?"

He chuckled and said with a little laughter in his voice, "No, but you're getting warmer."

"Good! My kind of meal. Ok, let's see…"

She walked into the kitchen. Again, he got lucky and timed it just right. It was done right as she walked in the house. He pulled it out of the oven.

She exclaimed, "Look at that great piece of work. Another one of those major food group meals, huh? That looks too good enough to eat. Can I frame it?"

He shook his head and smiled. "Sure thing. Then I'll just make another one for us to eat."

"Well, hold on there, my chef. Let's taste it first just to make sure it tastes as good as it smells." And it did. She was pleased.

As they were about done eating he suggested, "Hey, I think we should go out to the mall tonight for a little while. How does that sound?"

"Window-shopping is always at the top of my list of things to do." She said immediately.

When they were done eating, she hurriedly said, "Let me go upstairs and change. Then we'll hit the road. Don't worry about the dishes. I'll get them later! Just sit down and relax. Ok?"

He said 'ok', and off she went running up the stairs.

While she was upstairs, he cleaned everything in the kitchen, including the dinner dishes. After he was done, he sat down on the couch and waited patiently for her, pretending to relax. She came running down the stairs. *She always likes window-shopping. 'This was a good thing,' as she put it.* She turned and started for the kitchen.

"Ok, I'm ready to go. I just need to get a drink of water, then we can hit the…" She stopped mid sentence when she walked into the kitchen.

"Ok, I see someone didn't hear me about the dishes. Hmmm, Houston, we have a problem."

She poked her head out of the kitchen and stated,

"Mister..."

He looked at her and smiled. She shook her head. She couldn't finish the sentence. As he got up to go to the side door, he asked, "You were saying something?"

She put her arms around his neck and said, "Yes, thank you. You're pretty special. You know that, Brent?"

"Yeah, I know. I get that a lot!!!"

"Oh, you do, huh? Do I have some competition?" she asked while putting her hands on her hips.

"Well, you never know..." He stopped mid-sentence and started to laugh. He couldn't keep a straight face while looking at her.

"Grace, I'm only too happy to do it for you. So let's go and make some more memories." She smiled and hugged him. Off they went to the mall.

At the mall, they shopped until they about dropped. They came to a jewelry store. In the window was a beautiful silver watch. The face was a midnight blue with white fluorescent numbers. The date and moon setting features caught Brent's eye.

"Hey, look at this, Grace? Isn't it beautiful?"

"Well, I don't know about you, but if you ask me, the color is just perfect!"

"Well, I did ask you. Let's go inside and get a closer look," Brent stated as he started to walk into the store.

"Sure," she said as she followed him.

As he looked at the watch, he fell in love with the it. And before he knew it, his American Express Gold Card was on the counter. While he paid for the watch, Grace was looking at something in the glass display.

"Hey, look at this silver bracelet, honey. Doesn't it have a touch of class? Try it on for me to see how it looks on you." He looked at it and didn't say a word.

"Please?" she asked as she batted her eyes at him. "It won't hurt to try it for me, will it?"

At first glance Brent was not sure if he cared for it, but

after looking at it closer, he thought it seemed very classy. So he tried it on.

"Well, I think it looks great on you. It matches the watch perfectly." He agreed as he took it off.

"See, it was made just for you!"

"Well, dear, it might have been made for me, but I really don't want to buy it."

She then stated rather firmly, "Well, I didn't ask you to buy it now, did I?"

"No, you didn't."

"Good. I'm glad you're seeing it my way. Now I can check that one off too." Brent couldn't help but smile again.

He laughed and caressed her upper back with his fingers as he turned to walk out of the store. That touch ran a pleasant chill down her spine. It felt good.

"Are you coming?" Brent asked as he started to walk out of the store.

She took a moment to compose herself after his touch and then said very faintly to the store clerk, "I'll take it."

As Brent left the store, he noticed she wasn't with him. He turned around to look for her.

She took out her American Express card and handed it to the store clerk. "Honey, please wait a minute. Are you buying this? Why, Grace?"

"Brent, darling, I want you to have it. Please look at this. You can engrave a name on it if you wish. So if you have a 'SPECIAL SOMEONE' in your life that means a lot to you, you can engrave that person's name on it. Please take it, for me?"

Brent stood there thinking, *Well, after that sales pitch, how can I say 'no'?*

"Ok."

She continued, "Now you can engrave a name on it later if you want. Please put the watch and bracelet on for me. I would like to see you with them both on as we are out shopping. You'll look even sharper than you do right now, if that's possible. Now other women will see it on you too. But seeing you're with me, they will just have to look elsewhere for their own gourmet companion..."

Brent couldn't say 'no'. She helped him put both on his wrists.

They soon left the mall and went back to her house. As they pulled into the drive and got out, Brent spoke up,

"Hey, I have something special for you tomorrow night too. Is that ok with you?"

"Ok, dear. Don't tell me you are going to top tonight? I don't think I can handle that right now," she said with a laugh.

"No promises, my dear. By the way, thanks for the bracelet. I like it!"

They hugged good night, and he left for his hotel room. In his room, he took off the watch and bracelet and placed them on the nightstand. As he looked at them sitting there, his thoughts of her were so warm and appreciative - not only for getting the bracelet for him, but for everything she did for him.

What a lady! What will I ever do without her? He had a smile on his face as he lay down to go to sleep. He looked at the bracelet until he drifted off into a pure and different wonderland of dreams that electrified his heart and mind.

Chapter 13

When Brent woke up, it was 8:00 am. *Oh, great. She's at work already. I wanted to call her before she left for work.*

He tried calling her on her cell phone to wish her a good day at work and to tell her he'd be missing her all day, but her cell phone wasn't on. "Oh, well."

She mentioned last night that she was getting off early, or at least she was going to try to. Do I have a surprise for her or what? It's our last night together. So I'm going to make it a memorable one.

Wait until she hears her name being called over the speakers. I'm not sure if she's going to go hide or give me a kiss. Now that sounds great. Although, she might get upset. Oh, well. I think she'll just love it. I'm sure she'll go with the flow. There'll be some great wit and humor coming from her tonight about it I bet!

The day flew by quickly. On his way back to his hotel room from a friend's house, he decided to order some flowers to be delivered to Grace tomorrow, late Saturday afternoon, at her home after he was gone. *That will surprise her... I think.*

He pulled up to a florist shop and started to get out of his car when his cell phone rang. It was Grace.

"Hello... Kelly's Pool Hall. Odd Ball speaking!"

"Ah, yes. What time do you open today?" she asked.

"We open at 2:00 pm every day, ma'am."

"Well, I'd like to make a reservation for tonight," she said softly.

Brent held back wanting to say 'What kind of reservations are you looking for, baby.' He continued, staying professional.

"What reservations are you trying to make, ma'am? Not many people call a bar and asked for reservations..."

"Oh, well, I'm actually kind of new to all this bar stuff. I've got this dashing absolutely gorgeous man I'm going out with tonight. He just, well, shall I say, 'lights my fire'. And I want to make sure a pool table is available so we can be, shall I say, 'alone'. Do you think you can help me out with this sort of thing?"

There's that charm of hers. How does she do that so quickly? There's my heart again. She's got it and won't give it back. I'm not so sure I want it back either. I can't think of a response...

"Hello. Can you help me? Maybe we got disconnected. Ah, I'll just call back later, maybe."

"Excuse me, ma'am, I was serving a drink. I apologize

for not responding right away."

He started to laugh out loud. "I miss you, a little bit," he said sincerely.

"Oh, really? Well, how much is a little bit?"

Now it's my turn to be a tease. Let's see if I can push the right buttons to stir her soul like she does mine.

So with all the grace and acting ability he could muster, he started telling her how much he missed her. It was a performance worthy of Broadway.

"How much do I miss you? How can I count the ways when my soul is so lonely without you near me? How can I find comfort when you hold my heart in your beautiful hands? Is there any way to survive the misery and pain knowing you're not near me to cradle and to touch my life like you always do? Can there be a sun without a moon? Can there be a night without a day? Can there be good without having bad?" He paused and then continued.

"Hmmm, I must have lost the connection. I guess I'll try her later." He waited and she spoke up.

"Like heck you are. Keep talking. You're pushing all the right buttons, darling. I think you're piling it on too thick now. But I think it's great. Keep it up. This is a good thing, so I'm listening with both ears now. I know you don't mean a word of it, but it's so beautiful and its great hearing you say it. I just makes me..."

Makes her what... Ah, she's not going to say it. That tease again. What a lady.

"Makes you what, Grace?"

"Well, I could explain it over the phone, but I'm not as smooth with words as you are. So, I guess I'll have to just explain it to you in person. Hey, I think my cell phone battery is going dead. Hey, come by at 5:30 and we'll go out tonight. Ok?"

As he started to answer, he heard a dial tone. *Oh man, what a time for her battery to go dead.*

As she ended the conversation, a smile appeared. *That'll*

teach him to think he can outwit me. He might be able to sometimes, but I've had a lot of practice doing this. That will keep him thinking and wanting more...

She put the cell phone down on her desk. The battery was showing half-charged.

So, she is expecting me at 5:30, huh? Hmmm, I think I'll drive by her work and surprise her. She's not expecting it. So we'll see who surprises who... Brent smiled and went into the florist shop.

He walked around and picked out a nice arrangement that he thought she would like. A lady came by and asked, "Hello, sir. Can I help you?"

"Hi. I would like this arrangement. Can it be delivered tomorrow afternoon by a certain time?"

"Well, we can't guarantee it will be delivered at a certain time. What time do you want it delivered?" she asked.

"Between 5:00 and 5:30."

"I'm sorry, sir, but we close at 4:00."

Brent shook his head. The door opened and a lady walked in. It was the delivery driver for the store.

"That's our driver. She finishes up around 4:00 on Saturdays."

Brent asked, "Can I talk to her, please?"

"Sure. May I ask why?"

The driver approached the front counter. Brent asked, "Excuse me. Can I ask you a favor?"

The driver looked at Brent and responded, "What kind of favor do you want?"

"I would like to have this floral arrangement delivered to this address tomorrow between 5:00 and 5:30. I know you close at 4:00, but can you please deliver this tomorrow? I'll compensate you for your time and trouble." Brent continued in a soft, humble voice. "It means a lot me!"

The driver looked at Brent and didn't say anything.

"How much do you want?" Brent asked as he took out his wallet and pulled out a twenty. She didn't say anything.

He pulled out another twenty. She then spoke up.

"I think we can manage this delivery for you. I'll probably be out of uniform at the time because I'll be off the clock, if you don't mind."

"That's no problem. Thank you very much," he said with gratitude. "If she's not there, leave them at the side door. Ok?"

"Consider it done, sir." He paid for the arrangement and left.

He got into his car and smiled as he drove to her work. *She is going to be surprised when I show up at the receptionist's desk.*

Brent pulled up to the building where she worked. He got out of the car and stood with the door open, his left arm leaning on the open door and his right arm on the roof. He looked around and noticed the exquisite landscape around the building and the reflective magnificence the building gave to the entire area. He closed the car door and set the alarm. He walked up to the building and found the entrance. He walked into the building with an employee. He looked around at the beautiful lobby area. He checked to find what floor Grace was on and headed toward the elevator. It opened just as he got to it. He got in and pressed the button for the fifth floor. He watched the numbers change at each floor as the elevator went up. When it reached the fifth floor, it stopped and the door opened. He paused, stepped out and briefly looked around.

The reception area was elegant. It had a brownish style with gold- like metal trimmings. He approached the receptionist and placed his hands on the counter. She was answering phones and transferring calls. She looked up at Brent and gently held up a finger asking him to wait a minute. Eventually, she turned her head towards him and spoke.

"Hello, sir. How can I help you?"

"I'm here to see Grace. Is she available?"

"She is in. May I ask your name?"

"My name is Ramies, Brent Ramies. But I would like to surprise her with my visit. Is it ok if I just go to her office?"

"Oh, you're Brent. Grace has talked about you this week. Actually, that's all she has talked about. I see why! She was so disappointed she had to work while you were here. But when people are out sick, I guess we have to do what we have to do. She really is a very nice lady. I've known her for about five years. You know, she seems like she can be controlling at times, but she really isn't. She has a big heart."

"Wow, thanks for that tidbit of information. You sound like a commercial for her. So, she has talked about me, huh? I hope it was all good" Brent said with a smile and a touch of humor.

"Oh, yes. It was all good. Trust me..." she said with a smile.

"Her office is just down the hall on the right. Her name is on the wall by the door. It was so nice to meet you. I will have to ask you to sign in first, if you would, please."

As Brent signed in, he could hear some ladies whispering to each other. The receptionist got their attention and pointed to Brent. They stopped talking, looked at him and started to smile.

As Brent finished signing in, he said, "Well, thank you, ma'am. Have a good day."

Brent walked down the hallway towards Grace's office. He found it just as he was told. The door was closed. He knocked and waited for a response. He could hear a woman's voice inside the office. It sounded like she was talking on the phone. After a few moments, he heard, "Come on in."

He opened the door and saw her sitting facing the outside window, talking on the phone.

"I'll be with you in a moment, please." Brent didn't say a word.

She continued on the phone. "Yes, he's here. He's a

good cook and very thoughtful. I could bore you with more details about him, but I'll spare you. Actually, I wish he were here so I could have lunch with him. So that's about it. Hey, I've got someone in my office right now, so I've got to go..."

As she said that, she spun around to see who was in her office. Her mouth dropped open when she saw him.

"Hey, Mary, I've got to go. An incredible hunk of a man just walked into my office. And I don't think he's delivering Chinese food." She paused still staring at Brent. Brent just stood there smiling.

"Mary, he is standing right in front of me. I'll talk to you later." While still looking at him, she slowly attempted to hang up the phone. But she missed the base completely and put the receiver down on the desk instead. They could hear the voice on the other end of the phone saying, "What? He's there? I'll be right over. Don't go anywhere..."

She pondered if she should ask him how she could help him. "Hello, sir. If you're collecting for the Red Cross, I gave last month..."

She then smiled and got up out of her chair. They hugged for a few minutes.

"Hello, Grace. I just wanted to see you. How is your cell phone battery doing? Still not charged up?"

"Oh, that? Who cares... You are here now," she responded.

Do you have plans for lunch, Grace? If you don't, I'd like to take you out."

"Of course, Brent. I'd like to get out of here today. It's been hectic with so many people out sick. It seems like I'm working harder than ever."

"I'm sorry to hear that, baby. Let's go out and have a good time at lunch." They left arm in arm.

Down the hall came Mary, walking very briskly towards them.

"Hey, Grace? Are you going to introduce me?"

"Brent, this is my good friend Mary. Mary, this is

Brent!"

"Nice to meet you, Mary."

"Same here, Brent. I've heard a lot about you. It seems like you are the topic of the entire office."

"Well, I hope it's all good..."

"Well, to tell you the truth, all she does is..." But before Mary could finish, Grace flashed her 'THE LOOK'.

Mary started to laugh and said with a wink, "Oh, it's been all good!"

Brent immediately turned to Grace to see what she had done to stop Mary in mid sentence. Grace had wiped away 'THE LOOK' immediately and just produced a rather unique smile.

"I see. Well it was nice to meet you. You have yourself a good day."

"You do the same..." Grace and Brent said in almost perfect unison.

With that, they turned and walked out of the office.

They left the building and went to a restaurant to grab a bite. Before they knew it, it was time for Grace to go back to work. They headed back to the office, and he dropped her off at the entrance.

"See you after work," Brent said.

"You bet. I'm going to try to get off a little early today. After all, I'm not supposed to be working and it's Friday."

With that he got back into his car. "I'll be waiting..." He winked and drove off. Before driving off, he looked up and noticed a group of ladies looking out the fifth floor window. He waved, smiled and made his way out of the parking lot and onto the street.

Grace smiled back and turned to enter the building. She let out a big sigh. *I could get used to this sort of thing. I can't wait until I get off work.*

She happened to look up and noticed the crowd of ladies looking out the window. She just smiled and headed for the elevator.

She entered the elevator and pushed '5'. She closed her eyes for a moment enjoying the emotions her body was feeling. When the elevator door opened on the fifth floor, she opened her eyes. All the ladies from the office were standing around in the lobby, looking at her and smiling.

She walked briskly past them and back to her office telling them with a little bit of attitude, "He's taken!"

Chapter 14

At 5:00 Brent showed up. He pulled into the driveway and noticed her car was in the garage, but the garage door was still open. He got out of the car and made his way to the side door. He knocked and over the intercom, he heard,

"Yeeeeees????"

"I'm here, Grace."

"Come on in."

He walked into the house and said,

"Hey, honey. I'm home." *That'll get some type of reaction from her.*

She came out of the bedroom, leaned over the railing and said,

"Hi. I'll be down in a few minutes."

As she spoke, she noticed the tuxedo he was wearing. She went back into her bedroom and finished getting ready. Brent walked around and looked at her china cabinet. A few minutes later, she elegantly came walking down the stairs and up to him.

"I thought you were going to show a lady a good time tonight? I see you have your PJ's on. They looked pressed too! It looks sharp! But you're not going to go out looking like that with me."

He was puzzled and caught off guard by that remark. She said with a bright smile, "Here. Let me!" She reached for his bow tie. It was a little crooked. He shook his head and smiled. They hugged and smiled. As she hugged him, she noticed a rose in the hand that was behind his back.

"I see you've come bearing gifts of some type. This is interesting. Anything you wish to share with me?"

He noticed what she was wearing. Her black dress was stylish. It went just past her knees. It was elegant looking and looked simply gorgeous on her. His mouth opened some, and he couldn't do anything but clear his throat. He was absolutely taken back by her sheer beauty. Her hair was done up in a gorgeous manner. She just stood there patiently, waiting for a compliment.

After clearing his throat a few times, he humbly said, "As a matter of fact, yes. Well, you might look like a million bucks, but you're not going out with me looking like that either. That dress needs a little something."

She pulled her hands quickly to her hips with loosely closed fists. Then he brought out the red rose with the stem cut short.

"Normally, I would give you a corsage, but tonight I felt you needed something more fitting for the occasion."

He pinned it to her dress. She stepped back, and he smiled brightly.

"Did you mess up my tie when you hugged me? I hate going out with a crooked tie. I'm very self-conscience about my appearance."

She smiled and said, "It's perfect."

"Good."

Brent smiled back at her.

"Excuse me for starring, but I didn't realize you were royalty. As your humble companion, I'd like the honor of escorting you out for the night. There might be some trouble tonight, so where are your bodyguards? Will they be following us?"

She looked puzzled briefly, but smiled as he held out his arm so she could put her arm around it as they walked out the door.

He continued, "Well, let me explain. Seeing I have the

most beautiful lady in the world on my arm right now, I'm sure other guys will be hitting on you tonight... wanting a piece of the action, so to speak."

She smiled at him saying, "Well, I'm being taken out tonight by a dashing man who looks like a million bucks. By the way, I'm an old-fashioned gal. If you think you can sweet talk your way into my heart, think again. On the other hand, keep trying. You're hitting all the right buttons." She squeezed his hand and arm and leaned her head on his upper arm as they walked out of the house.

"The watch and bracelet look really good on you..." Brent just smiled.

"Oh, I see you noticed. Just remember, it's the man who makes the watch and bracelet look good, not the other way around!"

"I know..." she said in a commentary tone.

They pulled up to the front of the dance hall. The valet opened the car door for Grace and the other got the driver's door. Brent turned off the car and handed the valet key to the valet. They looked up at the entrance to the hall. It had huge wooden, gold accented doors. A person could see their own reflection in them. It gave the entrance an elegant touch of class.

They made their way through the doors and followed the music. As they got closer, the sound of the music became louder. The rhythm of the music stirred the soul as if inviting people to participate. They made their way to a table where they could sit and either order food or just enjoy the music. They sat together watching the band for a while. The band had just started playing the song "Time" (Clock of the Heart) by Mark Chesnutt. Halfway through the song, they looked at each other. They both were thinking the same thing. They didn't have much time left because tomorrow Brent was going home. They were both moving with the beat of the music. They started to get up to dance, but the waiter came by and asked them if they wanted a drink or if they were ready to order. They gave him their orders.

"Well, I don't know about you, but I'm looking forward to dancing with a dashing man tonight. Do you know anyone that might be interested?" she hinted.

He jokingly said with a straight face,

"Well, I really don't care to be dancing with any man myself."

She looked at him, started to smile and began laughing.

"But I would love to dance with you," he whispered to her.

With that, he stood up and asked, "May I have this dance?"

She offered her hand, and he gently helped her up. They danced to few songs while waiting for their dinner to arrive.

When the appetizers arrived, they returned to their table. They talked and even fed each other in a romantic way. Eventually, the main course arrived at the table. The feelings they felt toward each other were magnificent. Just like two peas in a pod. Whether it was rock-roll, easy listening, or whatever, the band continued to play as other couples danced. They finished their meal while enjoying each other's company - as they always did.

Soon they were on the dance floor again. When the music changed, they would change their style of dancing right along with it. They moved as if they had been dancing together for years. Finally, they decided that it was time to sit down and catch their breath. The music stopped for a little bit. What Grace was experiencing tonight would be memorable for the rest of her life. Brent hadn't told her what was going to happen next. Nor did he hint about it. "You know, Brent, you certainly know how to show a lady a good time. I'm having a marvelous time with you tonight. These days we've had together had been really great."

"I can say the same thing too. But this night isn't over yet. The surprise is yet to come."

As she began to ask him what he was talking about, he

excused himself to the restroom. About ten minutes later, the lead singer said,

"Tonight, folks, we have something special to share with you. We have a few new songs that we are going to play for you. What makes them so special is that we didn't write them. A gentleman here in the audience wrote the lyrics. We proudly attach these songs to the list of other fine songs we have recorded. The first song is dedicated to a 'marvelous lady', as he put it. Grace, will you stand up please?"

She looked around the room for another 'Grace'. Finally, she looked forward and pointed to herself. The lead singer nodded. She stood up slowly, wondering what was going on. She then began to wonder why Brent hadn't returned.

"This song was written and will be recorded just for you."

There were about fifty couples on the dance floor. They all looked back at Grace wondering who she was to get such special attention. As the music started to play, out from the back of the stage came Brent. As they continued playing, Brent started to sing,

> Have you looked into her eyes?
> And seen her wonderful smile?
> She has the look so wise.
> That warms you there inside.
>
> She's a Cover Girl, can't you see.
> She's a Cover Girl, at least to me.
> She's a Cover Girl, for all to see.
> She's a Cover Girl...
>
> As she walks on down the street.
> Every head will turn to seek.
> She impresses all she meets.
> With her glowing looks and charm.
>
> She's a Cover Girl, can't you see.

She's a Cover Girl, at least to me.
She's a Cover Girl, for all to see.
She's a Cover Girl...

When she enters in the room.
It's really charged with her there.
Her brightness really shows.
As she turns her head and smiles.

She's a Cover Girl, can't you see.
She's a Cover Girl, at least to me.
She's a Cover Girl, for all to see.
She's a Cover Girl...

I wonder to myself.
Who can capture her precious heart.
If anyone could be so blessed.
Having her so close to their chest.

She's a Cover Girl, can't you see.
She's a Cover Girl, at least to me.
She's a Cover Girl, for all to see.
She's a Cover Girl... (Music stops)

If you could see inside her heart.
Her strength is great to feel.
But her beauty is not what you see.
Because it's deep inside of her. (Music begins again)

She's a Cover Girl, cannnn't you see.
She's a Cover Girl, at least to me.
She's a Cover Girl, for all to see.
She's a Cover Girl, Girl, Girl... (Music and melody repeat)

What a Cover Girl, myyyy, oh my.
What a Cover Girl, so pretty to see.

What a Cover Girl, for the world to meet.
What a Cover Girlllllll, (Softly, low music)
She's a Cover, Girrrlllll....

As he was singing, her mouth dropped open. She had no idea he could sing. Some of the other couples sitting around at their tables started getting up because the beat was something they could dance to. Everyone was lulled to the dance floor - an invitation to come and enjoy the moment. Soon everyone was dancing, except for Grace. Tears started streaming down her cheeks, not only from the beauty in the words being sung, but also the beat of the music. He started to sing the chorus,

She's a Cover girl, can't you see.
She's a Cover girl, for all to see.
She's a Cover girl, at least to me.
She's a Cover girl....

After hearing the song, she was beside herself. The crowd gathered to the front of the stage showing their appreciation. They were chanting to hear it one more time. The band agreed to play it one again. They started the music, but Brent didn't sing. He raised his hand towards Grace and proceeded to jump off the stage and slowly walk to where she was sitting. The crowd slowly moved out of the way, parting them just like the ripple effect created by a boat's wake as it pushes through the water. His eyes never left hers. All eyes in the band and throughout the room turned to watch him as he walked towards her.

As he reached her table, the music slowly echoed into silence. There was a hush over the crowd in anticipation of something wonderfully romantic that was about to happen - something that would touch the hearts and being of all those who saw and heard it, not to mention those involved in it. The entire time, his eyes were fixed on her eyes.

He got down on one knee in front of her and slowly offered his hand to her to escort her onto the dance floor for this special dance together. She slowly offered her hand to him. He gently helped her up as the band started to play again.

He was wearing a wireless microphone and proceeded to sing the song to her while they were dancing. They didn't realize it, but they were the only ones dancing at the time. The other couples were watching with great interest what was going on in front of them and curious about what would happen next. They never saw anything like this before. Grace and Brent danced to the rhythm of the song and in timing with each other as if they had been dance partners forever. Halfway through the song, the rest of the crowd joined in trying to capture the moment for themselves. But as far as Brent and Grace were concerned, they were alone in the room. Brent never took his eyes off of Grace, and Grace was lost in his eyes throughout the whole song. When the song ended, he began to sing another one to her. She was so totally amazed at this point that she didn't know what to say or even think. She didn't need to say anything. He understood this marvelous lady that was a close and dear friend. There was no thought of tomorrow or of yesterday. It was just that moment. They both had the same feelings for each other. Soon the song was over.

"Mister Hunk. I didn't know you could sing?" she said.

"Well, I don't recall you asking me if I could," he said with a smile. "Did you like it?"

"Are you kidding? I loved it. It was a little embarrassing at first with everyone looking at me. But I got over it."

They left after the last dance, which was hours later, and he dropped her off at her house. He pulled up in the driveway, got out and opened the door for her.

"I'm going to miss these gentlemanly deeds of yours."

He smiled and gave her an innocent wink.

"I'm going to miss doing it for you, my dearest ...

friend." He almost said 'love'. But he caught himself before he finished. He walked up to the door, unlocked it and went in. He checked out the house to make sure it was safe for her to be alone. He came back, took her key off his key ring and handed it to her.

"Well, it's 3:30 am and we're both tired. I'll call you in the morning when I wake up. We can plan things from there."

She smiled and told him 'good night'. They embraced romantically. She closed the door and looked through one of the windows as he pulled out of the driveway and down the street, until the car was out of sight. She turned and slowly went up the stairs and into her bedroom. Before she took off her dress, she took the rose off and placed it softly on the nightstand where she could see it while she was lying in bed. She wished Brent was next to her.

Chapter 15

The next morning, the phone rang in his room.
"Hello!"
"Hey, are you still sleeping, Mr. Hunk? Did I wake you?"
"No. Well, yes. Hmmm, what time is it?"
"It's 11:45." His eyes instantly widened.
"Oh my gosh, I'm sleeping my life away. Sorry about that. I'll get cleaned up and be right over."
"Hey, do you need any help with that? I can make sure your socks match at least..." she said in a soft, really sexy tone.

He was stunned, but totally delighted by her charm. He let out a chuckle.

"Thanks. But by the time you get here, I'll be done and ready to go. Thanks for the offer though."

Not wanting to let the situation go at the moment, she continued.

"Where do you think I'm calling you from? Did you think to look out the peephole of your door? You might see something you really like. But seeing you're probably not interested..."

"Wait, dear. Hold on."

He dropped the phone and made his way out of bed and towards the door. But he wasn't really awake yet, and he got tangled up in the blankets and sheets and fell onto the floor with a thud. After a few moments, Brent realized he wasn't hurt ... except his ego. He got up and stubbed his toe. He was flopping around with the covers trying to get untangled so he could check the door to see if she was out there. Eventually, he got to the door and took a look with great anticipation, but there was no Grace. He walked back to the bed, stubbed his toe again on the corner of the bed, and tried to pick up the phone to talk to her. She was not there. All he heard was a dial tone.

Oh, man. What just happened to me? I'm dreaming all of this... Gosh, first my arm hurt and now my toe. I'm going to take a shower. Hopefully I'll feel better. He walked to the bathroom and realized he didn't have enough towels. He stood there shaking his head.

On my last day with her too! Hey, why did she hang up? Maybe I'm imagining all this. Hmmm, maybe her cell phone went dead. Oh forget it. I'm calling down for some more towels.

He did and about five minutes later, he heard a knock on the door and a female voice said, "Room Service. Here are your towels."

"Thanks. Put them right by the door. I'll get them in a minute." Brent got the shower going and went to get the towels. He opened the door and looked down. However, he didn't see any towels on the floor - only a pair of white tennis shoes and some legs attached. His eyes moved up the body to the pair of hands who were holding the towels and a smiling blonde lady. It was Grace.

Wow! Is this room service or what?
"Hello, sir. Here are your towels."
He froze for a moment. *Oh my gosh!* He just looked at her for a few moments. *She's so sexy just standing there.*
"Is there anything else you NEED, sir? Our hotel has a variety of other services we can offer if you need them!"
He just looked at her with a look she had never seen before. He reached out and slowly grabbed the stack of towels she had in her hands.
She continued. "Excuse me, sir. You look like you've seen a ghost or something."
"Oh, I'm sorry. Ah ... no. You just look like someone I know that I'm in town to visit. I'm very fond of her. You could be her twin. Your mannerisms are about the same. Anyway, thanks for the towels. It's appreciated. I've got to get ready so I can go see her."
With that, he closed the door and left her outside the room. He smiled as he went into the bathroom and hopped into the shower to clean up. He started laughing and smiling at the same time. Soon he forgot that his big toe hurt.
I got her this time. This is going to be interesting.
Grace was standing outside the door completely astonished at what had just happened. Her hands were made into fists now and were on her hips. She couldn't believe she was still standing outside his door.
What do I have to do to get into his room? I wonder if he can take a hint. What do you bet he's in there laughing at all this? Grinning from ear to ear. Hmmm, well, to be honest, I was playing mind games a little with him yesterday. And I suppose I deserve this .... nahhhhhh. Now the question is, do I leave or just wait for him to come out? Neither, I'm going for a can of soda. Now, where is the soft drink machine on this floor?
Brent hurried his shower and continued getting ready. Grace finally came back and knocked on the door. He went to the door and opened it.

"Oh, hi, honey. Come on in."

He gave her a glance and smiled. She shook her head.

He told her what happened after he dreamed that she had called to wake him. Now she was beginning to feel bad.

"I'm sorry I caused all that. Are you ok? Does it still hurt?"

"Oh, so it was you? Ah ... it's not your fault. I was just clumsy. Hey, guess what happened? You have a twin who works here at the hotel. Can you believe it? I called room service for more towels, and I swear this lady from room service came up that could pass as your twin. No kidding. I almost hugged her and invited her in."

He turned and went back into the bathroom smiling from ear to ear. *Yeeeeees,* he thought to himself.

She didn't say a word. She just sat down and waited patiently for him to finish up. He came out of the bathroom and began packing the rest of his things. As she got up to assist him, her eyes started to get moist. He noticed and stopped.

"Excuse me, I didn't give you a hug yet, did I?" They embraced for a while. She put her head on his chest. She started growing accustomed to his touch and comfort. It made her feel so secure and loved. She wanted so much to express these feelings to him, but she didn't quite know how. She wanted and maybe even needed to express them. But she couldn't. She needed a little more time to figure out how. She would know when the time was right to tell him.

They finished packing and left the room. After he checked out, they headed out of the hotel.

They approached his car, and he turned the alarm off. He opened the trunk, threw his luggage in and said, "Ok. Let me take you to your car. Are you hungry, dear? We can do lunch."

"I don't have my car. I took a cab. And, yes, I'm hungry."

Brent continued. "Oh. So you need a ride, huh? Well, let

me see here... Seeing I have room in the front seat, why don't I take you anywhere you want to go?"

Her thoughts drifted to what he had just said. *Anywhere? Hmmm ... As long as I'm in his arms, that's just fine with me.*

"Hey, I've got a better idea." He held the driver's door open for her. "I love being driven around by a beautiful blonde. So why don't you escort me to where we are going to eat, ok? I picked last night."

She hesitated about driving the car. He stood there patiently waiting for her to either say something or get in. After several minutes passed, he reached into his pocket and pulled something out.

"Will you give me your left hand, please?"

She looked into his eyes as she slowly gave him her left hand. He gently took it, placed an object into the palm of her hand and gently closed it. She opened her hand to find another penny, a penny for her thoughts.

"What are you doing to me, Brent? Normally, I know what I want when I want it. I'm in control. Now, I don't know what I want or don't want. And it's your fault. It seems like I'm so in..."

He moved closer to her and gave her a big hug. Her emotions were running wild now and she couldn't finish her sentence. And he knew it. He turned his head slightly and smiled.

"Thanks. I'm glad you feel that way about me. Remember the saying, 'live life without regrets? Life is about relationships and the experiences within those relationships?" He paused and then continued.

"Life isn't about this car, my house, my belongings, my career. It's nice to have them. But what is life about? It's about relationships. It's about people. It's about God and the Lord Jesus Christ! Your parents, your friends, your family, it's about all of that, Grace. Stop and think about it for a minute. Without family and friends, what does someone really have in their life? If they don't have a mate or don't take time to be with their mate and grow together, it's so very hollow. It echoes like an empty cave. There is no fulfillment in all that is done when one is alone. What difference does it make if you have everything and are not able to share it with someone close to you? I would give up all these things if I could share my life with someone! That is what is most important - well, at least to me."

He backed up and stood by the driver's door patiently waiting for her to take the keys out of his open hand. She smiled and held out her right hand with the palm facing up. He placed the keys into her hand and gently closed it while looking into her eyes.

"Have fun driving it and don't spare the horses as they say…!"

She got in. He closed the door for her and got in the other side. The engine roared to life, and she put it into drive. Then she floored it. The tires didn't make a sound. She stopped and asked him why.

Brent pushed a button on the dashboard and said, "Now floor it!"

She did. This time, the tires to made a loud screeching noise.

Brent chimed in, "It's called traction control. It gives the car more stability during acceleration! When you hear the screeching tires, you are not accelerating as fast as you could be because the tires are not making good contact with the road. Basically, they are slipping."

Grace stopped the car, pushed the button again and took off. The G force pushed them back in their seats. They smiled as they pulled out of the hotel parking lot.

"Yes, that's much better," she said with a smile.

The restaurant they went to was a nice one. They sat and ate a good meal. They talked, but the atmosphere was not a happy one. He was getting ready to go back home. They finished the meal and left for her house. When they got there, they sat on the couch for a while and spent the remaining hours together.

"Excuse me a moment. I'll be in the ladies' room."

She got up to go upstairs. He looked at his watch - it was almost 4:30 pm. Time was going by so fast.

I'm so comfortable here. It's almost like home because she's here. I love her style of decor.

He was starting to feel very sad because he had to leave.

There certainly wasn't enough time to get to know her better.

Maybe I should move here to be with her. But I have a great job and good career back home. As great a time as we have had, maybe it's just too soon to know for sure whether I should commit myself to her. Hmm, what's the rush? There's no one else in my life. But she hasn't really expressed that she wants to be with me over a longer period of time. I certainly feel the love from her heart and it's so nice. It could be just her charm and her personality who are so magnetic. But have I seen her enough to know what she's really like? Well, I've seen her when she gets home from work. I've seen her upset and venting. No real problem there. I had supper ready for her when she walked in the door. She likes my cooking too. Well, at least she said so. Maybe she's just being polite. I did the dishes and cleaned up the dinner table afterwards. I would do the same thing at home so that's no big deal.

His thoughts stopped as a raven flew by the window. It just stopped and hovered as if it were looking at him for a few moments. Then it flew off.

Well, unless she says something, I might as well just let it lie and enjoy it for what it was. I've got to get back, do my laundry, and get things ready for Monday. We've got a big project starting on Monday at 8:00 am, and I'm really needed there to make it work properly. We've spent months preparing for it. But now my heart aches because there is so much more I want to share with her. Maybe it's just not meant to be. There are a million things I can have in life. Then there are ten million things I can't. It's no fun accepting that, but hey, that's life. Deal with it. I have to think. I've been dealing with stuff like this all my life. This is just another chapter. But I want this so very badly... What good is it if I have all these material things and am lonely? Is a career worth a chance at possibly being with the love of my life?

His thoughts were interrupted by the sound of footsteps running down the stairs. He turned his head to see her brightness and that glow that filled the room when she was around.

"Ok, I'm back. So, what are we going to do now?"

She said that with so much energy and excitement. He marveled at her charm and spirit. She looked at him with a little puzzlement because he didn't answer right away like he normally did. She plopped down on the couch next to him and snuggled right up to him on his right side. Her head rested on his upper arm and shoulder. She put her left arm under his right arm. Then softly and gently she grabbed his right hand with her left one. She put her fingers through his and squeezed in an affectionate gesture. She grabbed her legs and propped them under her on the couch. She then placed her right hand on top of his hand and snuggled it. She saw the watch and the bracelet she gave him. He squeezed back three times. She felt it and looked up into his eyes. Then she realized and asked, "Is it that time already?"

His eyes become watery. She grabbed some tissue and wiped the tears from his eyes, which brought more of the same.

She cares so deeply for me. How can I ever leave her? She's so ... so precious. Now what do I do? I guess the right thing.

"Well, I've got a ride ahead of me yet. And it's best if I get...." He couldn't finish the sentence. His voice cracked as he tried to fight back the tears and emotions that were coming out through his voice. His heart was pounding with sadness. He wondered if she could hear it. He tried to speak, but couldn't.

Maybe if I say something to her, it could make or break it right here and now. Do I risk it? What do I do? I don't want to rush things if she's not ready. Maybe she doesn't really feel the same way. If she wanted to tell me something, then she would have told me already, right? But she hasn't, so I had better not force things. But my heart wants it so badly. Maybe it's because I'm so far away. But I would strongly consider moving here if she wanted to give it a try.

His thoughts stopped at the sound of her sweet, caring voice filled with energy. "Talk to me ... please. What are you thinking about, honey," she said.

She patiently waited for him to talk. He felt like he could take all the time in the world to answer. She made the moment, as she always did, so special because she cared about what he thought and his feelings as he did for her. Finally, he answered.

"I had such a fantastic..." Again, he couldn't finish his sentence because his voice started to crack from all the emotions he was feeling.

He looked down at her hands. Then, he placed his other hand on top of her hand and snuggled her hands as she continued to hold his. It was a sweet and tender moment as he started to think. *There is no feeling in the world like this. None. To love and be loved like this is so mind boggling. It hurts to realize I may never feel this way again.*

With that he raised her hands to his lips and kissed them gently. Her mouth dropped open in astonishment. The gentleness touched her heart like nothing had ever done before. Again, he made her heart race like he had done did so many times.

"I've got to go." With that, he slowly got up, still holding her hands.

She started to get up. He helped her gently off the couch. She looked at his chest and the rest of his body for a while. Her eyes eventually traveled up to his eyes. She asked,

"Where do we go from here, Brent?" He was slightly surprised but delighted by the question.

"I guess I probably should start looking in the local want ads. It might even be better if I talk to a couple of recruiters or headhunters here and find out about jobs in the area!" he said as he turned his head slightly with that boyish smile that grabbed and warmed her heart so much. His heart started to race. Maybe this was the signal telling him that she wanted more of a relationship with him.

She didn't answer ... as much as she tried, she couldn't. Her mouth opened slightly, but nothing would come out. *How do I answer him? Do I want to get involved with a man that's been through so many major hurts in his life? What if I hurt him? I know how I am. But he's seen that part of me too. I don't know. What's happening to me?*

She didn't give any sign that she was going to answer him. Her thoughts drifted back to many years ago when they began talking to each other. But now it became so much more than that. She still enjoyed the talks - even more now. But...

He waited, but felt there would be no answer at the moment. *Well, this is it, I guess. Maybe, for the time being anyway. Maybe I'm not the right person. Maybe I'm too nice. Maybe I should get angry. But why should I get angry with her? She hasn't done anything to get me upset. Ahhh, just let it go.*

He slowly released her hands, and she slowly released his. He started to walk to the side door where his car was backed into her driveway. She followed him. As he approached the door, she grabbed his muscular waist. She spun him around. She put her head on his chest and hugged him like he had never been hugged before. She wouldn't let go. He not only hugged her, but embraced her. His feelings for her ran wild in his heart as they always did when she hugged him. She made his heart feel so loved and warm inside. No one ever made him feel like that before. His embrace made her feel safe and secure like she had never felt before with anyone. As their hearts touched in the embrace, certain feelings were transferred between them. Maybe it was pure and true love for each other. The total peace and tranquility at that moment was incredible. Tears flowed from both of their eyes now. They looked at each other and wiped each other's tears away the best they could. They smiled together at that sweet gesture, for they were both thinking the same thing. They didn't let go of each other. Nor did they want to. They gazed into each other's eyes for a while longer without saying a word. They enjoyed the moment for what it was.

Then she got up on her toes and kissed him. He bent down to kiss her with his head turned slightly. After all this time, it was only the second time they kissed. So much was said, so much more was transferred, and even more was conveyed through that kiss. No words needed to be spoken after that. Two peas in a pod... They reluctantly released each other. He reached for the doorknob and opened it. He glanced back to see her eyes. She was looking down at the kitchen floor.

Oh no, I was hoping for one last look at them, maybe one last dip in the pool? It might be the last one for a while, or forever. You never know.

He walked through the door and closed it behind him. He proceeded to his car and opened the driver's door. He started to get in, but stopped. He looked up to see if she was watching through the kitchen door window. She was. Those beautiful blue eyes were now red from all the tears. She managed that beautiful smile and gave him a beautiful finger wave (her palm didn't move, but her fingers did ... all of them together as one). It was such a sweet little wave. It expressed the gentleness that was inside. He blew her a kiss good-bye. She acted like she caught it.

The car roared to life and started to move down the driveway. However, just before it reached the street, it stopped abruptly. You could hear a screeching sound from the tires as they locked up on the driveway. The car door opened. He jumped out and ran back to the side door as fast as he could leaving the car door wide open and the engine running. She saw him coming and opened the door. They embraced and kissed one last time, both crying uncontrollably. He went through the door one last time. He turned and smiled brightly at her. He wiped the tears away from her eyes with his fingers.

He tasted them and smiled saying, "I love you, my dearest sweetheart!" He waited a few moments. Her mouth opened in complete shock. Then he headed for his car and sped off. Her tears flowed in huge droplets as she put both her hands over her face. The tears flowed so quickly that four, then five, and finally, six streams of tears ran down her beautiful face.

Chapter 16

She turned away from the window as the car disappeared in the distance.

The house is so empty with him gone. I had such a great time with him.

She plopped down on the couch right where he had been sitting. She tried to feel his presence and essence that was left behind. She continued to cry uncontrollably until her body was shaking a little. After almost 25 minutes of crying, she realized, *What the heck am I doing here? Probably the most wonderful man in the world has just left my side. He told me he loved me, and I couldn't answer him. What's my problem? Get your act together, woman, and get with the program. I had the world in the palm of my hand with him here, and I let him walk out without saying a word. I had the privilege of having been loved in the past, and now I have the opportunity to be loved again, if I decide to take a chance and open my heart. Nothing is perfect. Just work it out. What do I have to*

lose? Am I nuts? Am I going to let him get away?
She started to say sternly, "NO, I'M NOT!"
With that she dashed out the side door and to her car. "Wait a minute, woman. Aren't you forgetting something a little important? It will be pretty difficult to drive your car without keys."
She dashed back into the house to get her purse and car keys. She left the house and opened the garage door. She got into the car and let out a sigh as her car started. She wiped away her tears and said, "Now let's go get my future! The man I love is only about thirty minutes ahead of me! Maybe I can make up some of that time!"
She pulled out of the driveway and headed for his house. As she pulled out onto the main street near her house and headed for the highway, another car was driving down her street and towards her house. It was the lady who was delivering the floral arrangement. That car pulled into her driveway. She got out, grabbed the flowers and headed for the side door. She knocked, but no one answered. She placed the flowers gently by the door and left.
The drive home was very depressing for Brent. The sun was out and shining. It was a nice, warm September day. He opened the moon roof to let some fresh air in.
Why can't I get comfortable? I just don't understand why? Brent pulled up to the tollbooth to get his ticket for the ride home.
He pulled away and accelerated. The car picked up speed very quickly while it thrust him back in the seat a little. It left every other car in its wake.
Ok, it's a four-hour trip. Again, I'm alone in my thoughts. But this time it's different. I can't find any comfort in those thoughts as I normally do. It seems my emotions are elevated beyond almost anything I ever experienced before. This is quite unsettling.
His heart was finally breaking from all the sorrow and pain he had experienced in his life. He grabbed his chest due

to the painful sensations that seemingly were tearing his heart apart.

Then he was reminded of all the years with Sue. How she would yell and argue over everything and nearly anything she wanted. There was tension around her all the time. All the stupid things she would bring up, to accuse him of, to blame him for - things that he had nothing or very little to do with. Yet, she was a master at being able to turn things around. She accused him of doing the same. But in the end, he never enjoyed the tone, the tension, the terrible atmosphere their relationship turned into the last years before she died.

It felt like all the memories were overpowering him. It was becoming difficult to drive. He was trying to adjust himself in the seat. But it didn't seem to help. He tried to turn on the CD player, but his fingers couldn't seem to push the 'on' button. So he tried to just sit and be comfortable.

I can't help thinking about this tremendous woman I left behind. For once in my life, I found someone who is the most charming and gentle lady I've ever had the honor of knowing. Plus, she is so funny. She understands. But I don't want to bring more grief into her life. Besides, with all this grief and agony I've experienced, what do I have to show for it now? How much longer is it going to continue to be like this? Will I ever get some relief from it? Questions, questions, and no answers as usual. But it's probably like that for everyone, I bet.

I guess I'll just spend the rest of my life alone. Why it is that most women don't want a man who's gentle, kind, and thoughtful? But they say they do. Does the sayings, 'if it's too good to be true, then it's not,' apply to this? That's mostly what women seem to think. Well, at least that's what they say. 'He's a jerk. He won't do the dishes, take out with the garbage, or help with the kids unless I nag him. After work, he thinks he can plop down on the couch and sit in front of the TV most of the night. Hey, I worked all day too. But he doesn't listen or care. Then there's baseball and football on the weekend...' That seems to be what most women say.

He was now becoming confused, bewildered, and saddened by all of these thoughts. He heard ladies talk like this for years.

But I'm not like that. I just want to share my life with her so we can do things together. I don't do these things for her because I have to, but because I want to. I want to help make her life easier because I love her. Why don't women see this? Oh, well. The only real thing I want in my life is to have a lady that show just a little respect for what I am as a man and love me just a little bit. Maybe that's asking too much. It doesn't look like that's going to happen. She doesn't have to be a beauty queen for me to think she is. I can't keep on giving myself freely like this. It's just too hard on my heart.

As the minutes turned into hours, he saw an Oasis in the distance. He looked at the clock on the dash.

Oh my, I'm less than an hour from home. But what am I going back to? There's nobody there to share my life with.

A very deep and lonely sadness started to settle in as he tried to sort things out. He noticed as he was driving along that the Oasis sign had advertisement that said, 'Soft Serve Yogurt.'

"Now that sounds good for a troubled soul like mine. I can use the restroom and get some yogurt in one stop."

Brent pulled into the Oasis, got out of the car and started walking into the Oasis. *I wonder if she's thinking about me.*

What Brent didn't know was Grace was only about thirty minutes behind him, and closing, on the toll road. And, she was thinking about him. *I'm not going to let him go. I don't care what he's been through. I'm miserable without him. I just want to share my life with him. Maybe I should call him on his cell phone? Why didn't I do that before I left? Well, I'm going to do that right now.*

'Beep beep' ... could be heard as the high-pitched tones echoed in her car. His cell phone rang four times. She heard the message, "Please leave a message after the beep." She hung up.

Inside the Oasis, Brent left the restroom and walked over to the soft serve yogurt counter. He stood and waited as the blonde lady behind the counter continued to clean with her back to him. Brent cleared his throat to get her attention.

She turned around, smiled and asked, "How can I help you, sir?"

Brent looked upon the lady and was shocked. His mouth dropped open a little. He couldn't say a word. He looked at her nametag, which said "Sherie." She looked about thirty five years old or so. He just stood there looking at her. She continued to look at him, waiting for him to tell her what he wanted. He didn't say a word.

"Sir, what can I get you?" she asked again in a pleasant voice. He tried to say something, but nothing came out. She started to turn around and do some more cleaning.

Brent gathered himself. "Ah, yes. Yes, I do. I'm sorry for starring. You remind me of a lady I know ... that I love. I wish I was with her right now..."

His eyes started to moisten up as he looked down at the counter in front of her. She paused for a moment.

"What's her name?" she asked quietly.

"Her name is Grace. I just spent a lovely four days with her."

"I see. Well, let me know if you want anything. Take as long as you need."

She grabbed the cleaning rag and started to wipe the counter in front of him.

"How about French vanilla? Make it a large and in a cone, please?"

"Yes, sir. Coming right up!" She filled the cone with yogurt and handed it to him.

"That'll be $3.59, sir."

Brent handed her a five, and she gave him the change. He put it in his pocket.

"Thank you, sir. And ah ... well, if I might say something, you never know what can happen! Have a nice evening!"

He looked at her in astonishment. Tears started to fill his eyes again. Brent said to her, as his voice cracked with the emotions he is experiencing at the moment,

"She said that a couple of times too. It seems to be one of her mottos."

She smiled and nodded.

"I would ask you what she is like, but it looks like you truly love her, and right now might not be a good time to ask that question."

He nodded his head, turned and walked out of the building to his car. He stopped and turned to look back.

Now, what are the chances of that happening? He shook his head and continued to his car.

Chapter 17

As Grace drove to catch him, she continued to ponder what to do.

Oh, great. He's not answering his phone. Oh, well. Maybe I should have left a message. No, he loves my voice. This is something I want to tell him live on the phone, if not in person. I could call him back and leave a message.... Nah, I want to surprise him. I know I can comfort him as he does me. Should I ask him to marry me? I think he's kind of old fashioned (just like me) on things like that, but I think I just might because he's so special. We'll be together for the rest of our lives. Maybe I should tell him I'm not going to take no for an answer. Gosh do I love him. I just love the way he cradles my hand when he holds it. I feel so ... protected.

She let out a sigh. *The way he opens the car door for me. How he makes me feel when we are together and even when we are not. How he escorts me through a doorway by holding the door open for me to walk through. Then how he very gently, while barely touching my lower back, guides me through the door, aahh, makes me feel special. What a man. I can't believe we have so much in common. He's so understanding and funny. Yet he gives me space when I need it. He listens to my whining and complaining when I need to get something off my chest. Sometimes he doesn't try to fix it either. This will be a big surprise for him when he comes home to his house, and I'm standing there waiting to embrace him with all my love.*

She smiled brightly. *I'm so thrilled just thinking about seeing him in a little while. Maybe I might see him on the road. Nah, with that car of his and its quickness, there is no way. So just be patient and drive. Don't go overboard on the speed. Don't want to have an accident or get pulled over by the police.*

In her hastiness to leave and be with him, she completely forgot to pack anything for the trip. The thought never occurred to her.

"I'm going to get him if it's the last thing I do. He won't be able to say no to me. I know he can't resist my charm. That's his weakness. And believe me, he's going to see a lot of charm coming up very shortly," she said out loud.

As Brent walked back to his car, he hit the remote alarm on his key chain. He got back into the car and almost dropped his yogurt.

Yeah, it's all fun and games until I make a mess with my yogurt. Who cares really? It's only a car after all. He turned on the ignition, and the engine roared to life. He put it in gear and accelerated quickly back onto the highway.

Now, this is nice. Having a vanilla soft serve yogurt and the wind blowing through my hair. This is good. It'll take my mind off my feelings for a while. Sherie put a nice curl at the top of the cone. Life sometimes is in the small details, the simple things in life. Wow a 15-minute stop too. Not bad, not bad at all. Too bad I have no one to share it with. I sure do miss her presence in the front seat.

Grace was now about fifteen minutes behind him.
The yogurt cone slowly disappeared. Soon, it was gone.
Now, I settle in and try to enjoy the short trip home.

Just over the bridge about a quarter of a mile ahead, the traffic started to slow down in both directions. The reason became clear almost immediately. A county sheriff's unit was sitting in the median between both lanes of traffic. Deputy Stan Ray was sitting in the unit watching the vehicles pass by. Soon he put his head down so he could do some of the paperwork from the previous tickets he had written that day. His buddy, Deputy George Atkins, pulled off the highway and stopped next to him.

George pushed the button and the driver's window started to go down. Stan's window was already down. "Hey, Stan, any excitement today? Catch any bad guys yet? Or are you just sitting here loafing on the taxpayers' time?" he asked as he chuckled.

"You would have known if I had, George. I would have called for backup and would have expected your sorry butt to show up and back me up. One thing is really funny. They think we're out here clocking them and we're just sitting here doing some paperwork and social chitchatting. At least they're slowing down."

Stan's little grin turned to outright laughter. George had to laugh too.

Stan continued, "Nothing but the usual cat and mouse game with these motorists. I heard there are some races in town. Business should be good this evening. Hopefully, I'll nail some of the foreign hot-rod idiots. I'll tell you, George, I'm tired of them coming to our town ... our area and putting other motorists at risk. I've seen so much death due to the recklessness of these speed demons. I will do anything I can to keep it from happening again, or at least lessen the amount of accidents that are caused by it."

Stan's voice started to rise as he was getting really

worked up. "Well, George, my lovely wife is moving out today and said she's filing for divorce tomorrow. How does that sound? I suppose, I don't blame her actually. In my line of work ... actually with all the close calls I've had with nearly dying ... well, I just don't think she can stand the pressure and stress of whether I'm coming home alive or not anymore. I guess you can say I'm a little worked up about it. Why did she have to get involved with a guy with a foreign sports car before divorcing me? I'd love to pull that guy over and show him who he's messing with..."

George had heard all of this before and was not surprised at what Stan was saying. The things they see and hear are not normal for any occupation.

"Maybe you should go in and call it a day, Stan. I don't want you out here getting into trouble because you are losing it. God knows there are times when I want to forget that there are laws out here that I have to follow."

"Yeah, I know, George," Stan said in an agreeing tone. But Stan was anything but in an agreeing mood. Internally, he was raging and it was growing by the minute. But, he thought he could control it.

George spoke up and changed the topic of the conversation.

"Guess who I saw a few weeks back? I ran into an old friend of mine from my college days, I kid you not. I pulled him over for a traffic violation. I was the best man at his wedding."

"So, did you give him a citation?" Stan asked with a grin on his face.

"No, but I gave him a run for his money before he realized who I was. I had him in handcuffs, had my hand on my gun. You know, the whole bit. I have to admit, it was a lot of fun. I scared the crap out of him. Hey, when we get together again, I'll have you come over and meet him. He's an alright guy. I'm sure you'll like him."

"Sounds good, George. But not anytime soon. I don't

feel like being nice to anyone right now."

"Hang in there, Stan. Don't lose your cool. Say, why not stay at my place tonight? The wife and kids are out of town for a few days. There's plenty of pop and enough food in the refrigerator to feed a small army. Help yourself and enjoy the cable TV. It might help get your mind off things."

Stan thought for a few moments and said, "Thanks, George. But I'm going to pass on that right now. I just want to be alone, I think. I'll settle down in a little bit. I'll be all right. I appreciate the offer though..."

"Well, please reconsider. You need a break from the streets, buddy. I don't want to have to come to your aid because you took your anger out on one of these motorists out here." George stated with concern in his voice.

"I'm going for coffee, Stan. Want to join me for a few minutes?"

"No thanks, buddy. I'm fine. I'm finishing up my paperwork. I'll just sit here for a few minutes and relax. Enjoy your break, buddy!" Stan answered back.

George said with a devilish smile, "Hey, how many of these motorists' hearts would really start beating fast if I pulled out of here suddenly with my lights on and quickly sped up behind somebody?" With that, George sped off with his lights flashing, chuckling as he went.

Stan put his pen down and thought for a while about his job, his life, the dangers that lurked around every corner, and what was ahead for him. *Some people are pure scum. They are out to get me, my position and what I stand for. What is my life?*

He thought about what he always wanted and what he could have had but didn't. *I really don't know what to do. Maybe George is right. Maybe I should call it a day. Wait ... I can't go home now. She's moving out. So much for that idea...*

Anger started to settle in. Deep in his mind, he wanted to take it out on somebody, but knew he couldn't. *I can still go*

to George's place. Maybe I will.
Let's see if I can relax in the seat just right, Brett was thinking. *Yes, that's it. I want so badly to call her, but I need to be patient. My exit is approaching in about ten miles.*
It was dusk outside now. The cool October air was fresh and crisp.
Let's see here ... should I call her or just wait until she calls? If she interested, I'll tell her I'll consider moving and give this relationship a try. I'll call just this one time. I'll try the home number first.
He accelerated and picked up the phone. He started to dial her home number but saw she had called him. His thoughts were interrupted when his cell phone rang. The caller ID showed it was Grace's cell phone. *Oh my... she's calling me. Maybe she's calling to say that she wants to give this relationship a try.* Brent was excited and nervous at the same time. The phone rang again and he answered it.
"Hello. Thank you for calling 'Premier Dating Services. Can I help you?"
"Yes. As a matter of fact, you can help me locate a dashing young man. His name is Brent Ramies. Do you know how I can reach him?
"Let's see ... I think he's in the database. Let me check. Here he is. I have a phone number for him. Would you like me to connect you right now?" he asked.
"Oh, please do!" she said with a positive voice.
"Here you go. Have a good day!" Brent made a couple of clicking noises as if the call was being connected.
"Hello. This is Brent." He said.
"Hey, Mr. Hunk. I thought I'd call you because I have something to tell you. Where are you right now? Are you at home sitting on your glider thinking of me?" Grace asked in a hoping voice.
Brent chuckled. "No. I'm still on the road. I'm not quite home yet. Why do you ask?"
"I was thinking after you left about one of the last things

you said to me. I sat on the couch, wondering why I couldn't respond to you. Well, I have a response for you. Do you want to hear it?"

"Well ... I don't know ... Well..." Brent paused and started to laugh out loud.

"Yes. Yes, I would like to hear whatever you have to share with me." Brent said quickly. Then he held his breath.

"Brent, I love you. But I want to tell you in person, that's if you don't mind."

Brent's mouth dropped open. Tears formed in his eyes. He felt that love from her, and it warmed his heart even more than before. He tried to answer quickly, but couldn't. He knew his voice would start cracking from all the emotion coming out. After a few moments, he composed himself and answered.

"Well, I suppose I can wait..." Brent paused. He couldn't hold back his emotional response any longer.

"I love you too, sweetheart. Thank you for telling me, honey. And, yes, I would love to hear it from you in person. I suppose I can turn around and come back to your house. I'm probably about three hours or so away. Do you want me to come back, Grace?"

"Well, Brent. I have a better idea. Exactly where are you right now?" she asked.

Brent told her. "Why do you ask? Wait, wait a minute. Where are you right now, darling?"

Grace told him where she was and then added, "Would you like to meet at a truck stop or somewhere along the highway?"

Brent's car passed by Stan's unit.

His excitement grew. "You are where? No way... Wait. We can meet at my place. No. I don't think I can wait that long. There's an Oasis just ahead of you. It's the only one in that area, so you can't miss it. It's about ten minutes away from where you are right now. How about I meet you there? I'm maybe ten to fifteen minutes away from there."

"That's the best plan I've had for many hours now. I love you. I'll see you there. I can't wait until I see you, Mr. Hunk."

"I can't wait to see you too, Grace. You've made me so happy. I guess we are like two peas in a pod now. Be careful driving, honey. I love you." Brent hung up the phone.

She said she loved me and came out all this way to see me. I can't begin to express how happy I am right now. Now where can I turn around? Hmmm ... there's a median turnaround in the middle of the highway just ahead. If I use it, I can beat her to the truck stop. Maybe I should just go to the next exit to turn around. But that's another seven miles down the road. I can't wait that long. What's that saying, 'You only live once.' Hmmm....

Grace put her phone down on the seat. She was so excited about telling him she loved him. It was like a huge weight was lifted off her shoulders. *I get to see my man. Oh, this feels so great. I can't wait.* She looked at her watch - nine minutes to see him.

The minutes passed by rather quickly. Soon she saw the Oasis ahead. *I bet Brent is already there. My guess is he's standing outside waiting for me. I'm sure he'll try to open the door for me. But I don't think I can wait that long to feel, to hug him as hard as I can. I just need to remember to put my car in park when I pull up.*

Grace pulled into the Oasis. She drove around looking for Brent's car, but didn't see it. Disappointed, she pulled into a parking space near the entrance of the Oasis because the parking lot was nearly full. A sheriff's squad car was parked right next to her car. It was a convenient spot for her to be able to watch who pulled in. *Hmmm... he said he was only ten minutes away. It's been a little over ten minutes and he's not here. Maybe he underestimated how far away he was.*

Stan had his radar out checking for speeders. He clocked a car, pulled out, and accelerated to catch up to it. As he caught up to it, he turned his flashing lights on. *That car looks familiar. I wonder if that's the jerk who's having an affair with my wife. It sure looks like the guy I saw several weeks ago walking out of my house. Probably making love to my wife in my bed and having the guts to park his fancy car right in front of my house. I wonder how many times it was parked there. I bet the neighbors saw the car there regularly. That's it. I'll pull his ass over and show him what happens when you mess with a cop's wife.*

Stan picked up his radio and told the dispatcher where he was located. He continued, "Dispatch, I want to run a plate. It's a dark-blue BMW, plate number Mary, Yellow, Frank, Robert, Thomas, Bob, Mary, White."

The dispatcher repeated it back to Stan correctly. He put the radio down.

The dispatcher responded to Stan's inquiry telling him, "The car has not been reported stolen. There are no wants or warrants for the owner."

"Thank you, dispatch."

The driver of the car looked in his rearview mirror and spotted the police car behind him with its lights flashing. The driver turned on his blinker to let the officer know he was pulling over. Within a matter of a few seconds, both cars were stopped on the side of the road.

George walked out of the Oasis with a cup of coffee in his hand. He noticed a car parked next to his unit. The blonde lady sitting in the car was looking towards the entrance as if she was expecting someone to show up. The situation looked a little suspicious with her sitting there looking around.

George walked over to his vehicle and started to approach the driver when he heard the crackle of the radio and the voice of his buddy, Stan, calling in his location and the plate he wanted run. George stopped next to his car and began to ponder. *That car sounds familiar. Hmmm... Oh no... I wonder if that's the car that was parked at his house. And if Stan pulled him over, Oh my, this isn't good. With the* condition he's in, this may not turn out for the best. He's not far from here. I'd better get there to make sure Stan doesn't do anything he'll regret later.

George threw his coffee down on the ground and jumped into his unit while giving a fleeing glance to the lady in the car next to his. He took off squealing his tires as his car gained speed very quickly.

Grace was sitting there watching the officer as he appeared to start to approach her. She heard the conversation over his radio. *Hmmm... Another BMW. There are a lot of them around here. I know Brent has two of them.*

She continued to look around for a few minutes waiting for Brent. Then she started to worry. It's starting to get dark now. *Where is my love? He's running late. I wonder why? Wait, wait a minute. What was that license plate I heard over the sheriff's radio? Let's see, "Mary, Yellow, Frank, Robert, Thomas something. Think, Grace, think.*

She scrambled to get a piece of paper and pen. *Ok. Write it down...*

Mary, Yellow, Frank, Robert, Thomas, Bob, Mary, White. Let's see, MYFRTBMW. Oh no. My first BMW. He got pulled over I bet. Poor guy. No wonder he's late. If he's not here in two minutes, I'll call him on his cell phone.

Stan got on his loud speaker and said, "Get out of the car and walk over to the other side of the car very slowly. Keep your hands where I can see them."

Brent started to wonder as he put his car in park. *Now, that's strange. Is this George again? Is he up to no good again?*

He got out as he was instructed. Stan got out of his vehicle as Brent stood off to the side of his car. The spotlight from the unit illuminated the interior of Brent's car. The officer brought out his flashlight and turned it on. He looked inside the car to see if anyone else was inside or if anything in it looked suspicious. He then focused his attention on Brent. "Sir, put your hands on the top of the vehicle and spread your legs."

Brent complied with the officer's wishes. As he put his hands on the roof of the car, he heard his cell phone ring. The caller ID showed that it was Grace. *Oh great! I'm late. Isn't this just wonderful? I'm enjoying one of the happiest times in my life. And what happens? I get pulled over. I guess I should have met her at my house. Oh well, this shouldn't take too long - I hope.*

Grace got Brent's voicemail. *He's not answering his phone. Something is wrong. Hmmm... I'm going to drive down the highway and see if I can find him. He should be on this highway. The officer may not let him answer his phone.* She started her car and headed to where she thought he was.

Brent started to ask if he was going to be arrested, but stopped when he felt the officer's heavy flashlight strike the lower part of his back. He swung it hard and hit Brent's spine dead center the blow. Brent's whole body screamed and rocked with pain. Then, he was struck again. This time, he was struck him in the back of the thighs with the same brute force.

On the other side of the highway, Grace noticed the cars starting to slow down. She looked to her left to see what was going on. She noticed both of the cars and the struggle going on between the two of them.

"OH MY GOSH! What's going on over there? That looks like Brent's car. I've got to turn around."

Brent was stunned. *My gosh, he's going nuts. He's trying to kill me. I can't let that happen.*

His thoughts turned quickly to Grace. Somehow, he mustered up enough strength from his screaming body to turn around and give the officer a few judo moves. Within about ten seconds, the officer was on the ground, face down, with an arm behind his back. Brent quickly pulled out the officer's handcuffs and put one on his right wrist, which was behind his back. Then Brent put the officer's left hand in the other handcuff. His hands were now immobile. When Brent was able to control the pain from the two strikes he had received, he turned to the officer.

"Why did you do this to me?" Brent asked as he helped the officer up and leant him against the car.

"You're the jerk who's having an affair with my wife. Did you think I wouldn't find out? You yuppie rich 'Professionals' make me sick." Then Stan spit on Brent's shoe.

Brent shook his head. He put his hand on his lower back trying to bring some relief to the pain. "I don't know your wife. What are you talking about?"

"Don't try to deny it. At least be man enough to admit it." Stan said with much disdain.

Brent turned away from the officer briefly. As he did, Stan slowly started to reach for his weapon. He almost got his hand on it when Brent noticed and said, "I don't think so. Now I'm going to slowly take the gun, remove the bullets, and throw it off to the side so you can't get to it. I'm not going to shoot you."

Brent proceeded to take the gun. He turned the gun up and away from both of them and proceeded to drop the clip that was inside it. He had lowered it halfway when a second unit came to a screeching halt about ten yards away. Brent was startled for what seemed like an eternity. Out of the car in a flash came another police officer. Then Stan yelled out loud, "HE'S GOT MY REVOLVER! HE'S GOT MY REVOLVER!"

The second officer heard this and yelled back sternly, "SIR, PUT THE WEAPON DOWN NOW!"

As Brent started to drop it, the second officer repeated the words in even louder, "SIR, PUT THE WEAPON DOWN NOW!"

As the gun started to leaves Brent's hand, a bright silver reflection came from Brent's bracelet and flashed across the second officer's face. The sound of a car backfiring could be heard. Then, a couple of shots were fired by the other officer.

It too sounded like firecrackers going off.

Both shots hit Brent in the stomach. The gun Brent had in his hand dropped to the ground. He almost immediately fell down to his knees. Brent was in a daze. He moved his hands to his stomach as he started to feel the pain. He looked at his hands and then at his stomach. Blood covered his hands and shirt. He looked up at the second officer who was approaching him in a crouched position with both hands on his gun. His revolver was aimed at Brent's head. Brent started to make out the face of the officer who was approaching him. He fell to the ground to one side, and then onto his back.

The stars are so beautiful tonight. Will that be the last thing I see here on earth? Gosh, I never thought how cold the pavement could be at night.

The officer who shot him appeared right over him with his gun drawn and pointed right at his face. The officer kicked the revolver out of the way.

Oh, my gosh. It's George Atkins, my best man at my wedding many years ago.

George absolutely couldn't believe his eyes. "Brent, is that you?" George asked.

"Yep, it's me, George. I've got to hand it to you. You're a good shot." Brent commented.

"What is going on here, Brent?" Confused, he lowered his gun, but still kept it in his hand. He knelt down beside Brent.

Brent told George what happened after he was pulled over. George turned to Stan. He didn't say a word. Brent could see tears forming in his friend's eyes as he said, "I'm so ... I'm so ... sorry. I'm calling an ambulance now. You lay still and try to relax. I'll get help on its way."

Brent raised his hand up to George's forearm and gently grabbed it. "Don't bother ... we both know what happens with these types of wounds..."

Their conversation was halted for a brief moment when

they heard the screeching of tires against the pavement around them. About twenty yards ahead of them, a car came to a sudden stop. About five seconds later, a woman jumped out started heading towards them. George started to get up and stop the driver from coming any closer. Brent grabbed his hand and said, "George, don't leave me now." George didn't.

"This isn't your fault. You were doing your job." Brent added.

"Brent, I discharged my revolver because I saw a flash of light and thought you were firing a weapon at me."

Brent shook his head in understanding. "I figured that was the case. I just bought this silver watch, and this silver bracelet was a gift from a lady friend of mine. I bet you thought it was a gun for a moment, didn't you?"

George nodded.

Brent continued. "It's too bad you'll never get to meet her. I think you would have liked her. She's so incredible, George. She most certainly is. I wear the bracelet on my right wrist because I always held her left hand. I was supposed to meet her couple of miles down the road at the Oasis about ten minutes ago. I bet she's a little worried that I'm not there yet. She called me right after I got pulled over." Brent paused and then continued.

"You know, my friend, it's not often the best man gets to gun down the groom years later…" he said with a little chuckle.

George couldn't say anything, but shook his head slightly.

The pain was increasing now. "Hey, you're an ordained minister, George. Is this how you perform a shotgun wedding?"

The tears started to flow from his dear friend's eyes now. They ran down his cheeks and onto Brent's arm.

Their conversation was abruptly stopped by a different voice coming from down the road. It was the other driver, a woman.

Chapter 18

As she approached, Brent started to recognize her voice. It was Grace. As she got closer, George started to get up to stop her.

"Don't. I know her. I think that's Grace, the lady I was telling you about. Please, let her come."

George wasn't sure if he should let her near Brent or not. George always did look out for Brent. Seeing this might be his dying wish, he backed away a little to allow Grace to see him.

As he backed away she ran up demanding, "I think I know the driver of this car.... Oh, NO! Is that you, Brent? What's going on here?"

She looked down as Brent lay there in a pool of his own blood. She let out a scream. "You're bleeding... all over the ground. What happened? Why are you bleeding? Who did this? Get a blanket to keep him warm... NOW. There are a couple of blankets in the trunk of his car. We've got to stop the bleeding."

She knelt down by Brent. "Oh, sweetheart. Does it hurt? I'm sorry, what a dumb question to ask."

Brent shook his head and said, "Yes, baby, it does."

"Oh, please, someone call 911." she yelled.

George grabbed the other gun and placed it inside his belt after checking to make sure the clip wasn't in it and the safety was on. He walked over to Brent's car and got out a blanket. He called for an ambulance on his radio.

Grace's eyes turned to Brent's. The reflection and angle of the headlights made her eyes look even lovelier than he'd ever seen them. "You're so absolutely beautiful. I love you, my dearest love! Just let me gaze into your beautiful blue eyes."

She bent down to gently cover his mouth with her

fingers. "Shhhh ... save your strength, baby. Help is on the way. I'm here now, and I'm not leaving you alone again, ever. I want to spend the rest of my life with you, my love. We'll work out the details. Just relax the best you can and the ambulance will be here shortly. Ok?"

She gently felt where he was shot. He grimaced in pain. Her heart panicked and terror started to flood her soul. She was kneeling right by his stomach. As she looked back into his eyes, the tears fell from her eyes like a river flowing down a mountain. She bent her head down close to his. Her tears dropped onto his face. He opened his mouth to catch a few of them. They tasted sweet and salty. Then he smiled.

"You crazy man, my man. Did you just catch my tears in your mouth?" He just smiled.

She smiled back, turned on all her charm and asked, "Will you marry me, sweetheart?"

George walked back to where Brent was lying. He placed a blanket on him.

"I radioed for an ambulance." George stated.

Tears flowed from Brent's eyes now, streaming down the sides of his face and into his ears. He smiled and said in a joking tone, "You picked a romantic setting for this great event... of course I will, baby. I would love to cuddle with you in bed and hold you tight as you go to sleep with your golden blonde hair in my face. I look forward to being able to wipe your tears away if you let me. We can share our triumphs, our failures, our happiness, and sorrow, the good times and of course the challenging ones. I want so much to just sit near you and share in your presence, your essence. To see you smile, to hear your jokes and laughter. I love your humor so much. You are the most precious lady I've ever known. I must apologize though. I don't have a ring to give you right now. Will you accept my new watch until I get you a ring?"

She smiled and accepted the watch as he slowly tried to take it off. He struggled but was able to get it off with her help. She was going to say something, but changed her mind and shook her head in amazement. *Here he is lying in a pool of his own blood, and he's worrying about my ring? That's Brent though. Always looking out for me in the little ways.*

His words were now coming out more slowly and with great difficulty.

"My love, don't blame George for what happened. By the way, he was my best man at my wedding to Sue. We were friends back in college. We still are... You know, as I was driving home, I was thinking a lot about you. I even saw someone at the Oasis that looked a lot like you."

Now the choking started. Her tears flowed even more. She started to realize he wasn't going to make it. But she wouldn't accept it. Her body began to shake some as he continued to speak.

"I realize I'm not dressed for success at the moment with this mess all over, but would you give me one of your hugs please?" Brent asked. "They always ease my pain."

She smiled and cried even more. She bent down and hugged him as dearly as she always did. Despite the physical pain it caused, it felt so good to him.

"Where is that ambulance?" she screamed as she turned her head away from his while crying. "I want that ambulance here right NOW!!! DON'T JUST STAND THERE AND WATCH HIM DIE LIKE THIS! YOU'RE HIS FRIEND! DO SOMETHING..."

The pain, the anguish, the misery, the sorrow, the hurt, and pure loneliness struck her like a cold wind on her bare in sub-zero weather. A knot was forming in her stomach. It kept growing and growing. Then it got tighter and tighter until she started to experience pain like she had never experienced before.

He was starting to struggle now, yet said,

"Honey, I'm so sorry I got into this mess. I'm sorry I didn't make it to the Oasis. I guess I should have met you at my house, huh? But I was just so excited to see you that I didn't want to wait. It looks like I messed this one up. I didn't think turning around in the median could cause such a problem. I guess that was the wrong choice. Looks like this is my destiny. Or ours?"

He managed to wipe away some of her tears as she grabbed his hand and held it to her face. His touch on her face felt as romantic and passionate as it always did. He continued.

"I love you, dearest. My heart is singing now because you are here." She cried and laughed at the same time.

She kissed his hand and said, "I came out here to tell you 'I love you and want to marry you.' And I wasn't going to take 'no' for an answer. I left in such a hurry that I just realized I don't have any clothes other than what I'm wearing."

She smiled as he said. "I never saw you without clothes. I wish I had, dearest baby."

She turned her head slightly and flashed him a tender and loving look that lit up his face so brightly. She caressed his face ever so lovingly with her hands. "I have the same wish too, my dearest."

The coughing came more frequently now. His eyes started to close as the pain was becoming more unbearable.

A thought hit her like a ton of bricks. *I might have been able to prevent this from happening. Why didn't I tell him I loved him before he left? I could have asked him to stay a little longer. He might have stayed longer or even the night with me. We could have bonded together more this afternoon. Maybe I should have called him before I left the house. Oh no. What have I done? Oh, God, please don't let this happen. I'll never forgive myself if he dies...*

Her thoughts were broken by the movement as he started to shake and convulse from the pain that was racking his body.

"I'm here, honey. I'm here. Let me ease your pain. I've got you. Don't leave me. Please don't leave me. It'll be ok, darling. Honest it will. I'll take good care of you. Don't worry about a thing! I'm so sorry I didn't tell you I loved you back at my house! Please forgive me. I might have prevented this. Oh NO! This isn't happening. No, it's not. You're mine. You're staying here with me. Oh please, oh please, PLEASE...."

She grabbed him, put his head in her lap and started to rock back and forth. Her internal pain and anguish reached well beyond fever pitch now. He felt her anguish that ran so deep inside her soul. She had never felt pain like this before. It seemed to get worse and more intense by the minute. Somehow, Brent managed to open his eyes one more time.

"Sweetheart, it's not your fault. There is nothing to forgive. You didn't do anything wrong. I used that turnaround illegally, not you. I caused this."

Her clothes were soaked in his blood now, but she didn't care.

He struggled to say "I think this is it, honey. I'm so sorry fate had this happen to us. I wanted so much to live our lives together. Words can't begin to express how I feel about you. I think we would have made a great team. I respected you from the very first moment I saw you so many years ago. I love you..."

He tried to continue, but just smiled as more tears streamed down his cheeks. Then his body began to shake uncontrollably. He could barely speak.

"I'm so cold now ... it's freezing here. Can you turn up the heat some?" She couldn't help but chuckle and hurt all at the same time because he said it in the humorous way that only he could do.

"If it's not asking too much, Grace, can I kiss you one last time please? Can I swim in those luscious eyes of yours one last time?"

Her gorgeous eyes connected with his. "You can do anything you wish, my soul mate," she said with a beautiful smile.

As she bent down to kiss him, he said, "I love you, Grace!"

They looked passionately into each other's eyes. Then their lips touched softly and tenderly as they shared their last moments together. It looked and felt like time stood still as they blocked out the rest of the world for that ninety seconds. Somehow he managed to get his arms up and around her to embrace her tightly one more time with the last ounce of strength he had left. He saved that last ounce just for her. Though she couldn't see it, when he wrapped his arms around her that last time, he clutched the silver bracelet she gave him. She felt him embracing her like he always did in the past. Those long, strong arms of his would make her feel safe. Then the embrace stopped. His lips started to slowly withdraw from hers. His arms started to go limp like the rest of his pain-racked body. They fell upon the pavement with the palms facing up. His head fell slightly to the side.

"No, no, no, no, no, no, you are going to be ok. Brent... you, you... YOU CAN'T LEAVE ME LIKE THIS..." she said as her voice started to rise higher and higher. She started to give him CPR. Over and over again. Finally, George knelt down and touched her shoulder.

"No, George. I'M NOT GIVING UP. HE'S NOT GOING TO DIE. HE'S NOT. DID YOU HEAR ME, HE'S NOT, HE'S NOT..."

George gently reached down and felt for a pulse on his friend's neck. He pulled his hand back. Grace slowly looked up into George's eyes and noticed the tears streaming down his face. His life would never be the same. He just ended his friend's life. He stood up, looked at Stan and gave him a stare. His anger started to rise, the longer he looked at Stan. He slowly and deliberately walked over to Stan, who watched the whole scene in handcuffs. George was so angry, his hands began to shake.

"This is the reason I wanted you to get off the streets. Because of you wanting your vengeance, I've just shot my long-time friend. I LOOKED OUT FOR HIM LIKE A BROTHER. I WOULD HAVE GIVEN MY LIFE TO SAVE HIS... DO YOU HAVE ANY, AND I MEAN ANY IDEA HOW I FEEL NOW???

George paused for a moment and whispered in an even more intense tone,

"Stan, I'm this close to releasing onto you the same INTENSE vengeance you have for the man who is having an affair with your wife. You so much as say a word that I don't like or give me even a hint of attitude, I'll send you to meet your maker... Do... you... understand... every... word... I'm... saying... here... Stan?"

Stan nodded his head and looked down to the ground.

George paused and asked while walking away, "Was it worth it, Stan?"

Stan didn't say a word. George turned and walked over to the edge of the highway where there was a gully for rain water to run off the highway. Beyond it was a lake. He looked at the trees that were lined up like soldiers in the forest. George slowly took the badge off his shirt. He placed the star in his hand, turned, and looked at Brent's lifeless body. He squeezed the star as hard as he could. As he was squeezing, his hand began to shake. Then blood began dripping from his hand as the points of the star pierced his skin.

"I'll never do this again." He turned and threw the badge as far as he could throw it. That was his last day as a deputy. A part of him died that day with Brent.

Grace, after watching and hearing what George had expressed to Stan, looked away from George. She looked back down into her soul mate's face and noticed his eyes were still open. She took her fingers and gently closed his eyelids. She again grabbed onto him and held him tightly. She started to shake even more. She clutched the watch. All the memories of them together, the hand holding, the door openings, the dinner dates, driving around in his car, having the time of their lives together, sitting and watching TV, making fun of some of the shows, all the jokes and laughter, the songs he wrote and produced just for her. One of the songs echoed in her heart and mind

'In time, it could have been so much more. This time is precious, I know. But you and me, we know we got nothing but time...'

All this flashed across her mind within a matter of seconds. It came so fast that she literally couldn't stand another second of it. It felt like her heart was about to literally burst inside her. With all the anger and strength she could muster and with a blood-curdling scream that could be heard from well over a half-mile away, she cried while looking up,

"NOOOOOOOOOOOOOOOO!!!!"

One pea in the pod...

Made in the USA
Charleston, SC
08 January 2017